MUSE OF THE WITCH

DEANNA CHASE

Editing: Angie Ramey

Cover image: © Ravven

Bayou Moon Press, LLC

www.deannachase.com

Printed in the United States of America

ABOUT THIS BOOK

Wanda Danvers is always the life of the party. She sets her own terms and answers to no one. Her love life is no exception even if she is dating the talented and handsome Cameron Copeland. But before things can really take off, her teenaged step-sister shows up on her doorstep, needing a place to stay. Now with a teenager to care for, dating is complicated and so is Cameron. Suddenly he's asking for a commitment… something Wanda has vowed never to give.

Cameron Copeland knows what he wants. And what he wants is Wanda Danvers. He's ready to settle down, but how can he convince the commitment-phobic woman of his dreams he means business when he's always traveling out of town for work? Add in a troubled teenager to the mix and Cameron has some serious work to do. But just as he's ready to show Wanda he's worth the risk, his gets a surprise visit of his own. Is it all too much for both Cameron and Wanda, or will they find a way to finally make a family of their own?

CHAPTER 1

"You were wearing *what* when his parents walked in?" Abby Townsend gasped out. A lock of her long blond hair fell out of her messy bun as she threw her head back and laughed.

"A see-through camisole," Wanda said with a grimace. She still couldn't believe that Cameron's parents had walked in on her while she'd been waiting in his room at the Keating Hollow Inn, ready to rock his world. He was a screenwriter who'd come to Keating Hollow recently to work on his latest project. After Wanda and Cameron had gotten together, they'd had a couple of hot weeks before he'd taken off to work on his latest movie. But he'd texted to let her know he'd be back in town that night and she'd decided to pick up right where they'd left off… Except his parents had clamjammed her. "That's the first time I've ever met a man's parents with my nipples on full display."

"Oh my gods." Abby clasped a hand over her mouth and shook her head while tears of laughter pooled in her blue eyes. "That's one hell of a way to make a first impression. What did you do?"

"What do you think I did?" Wanda took a long sip of her beer and stared up at the star-filled sky. When Wanda had run from the inn, she'd gone straight to Abby's and talked her into an evening ride on Wanda's party-mobile golf cart. Normally they'd ride around town with Prince blaring from her sound system, but that night they ended up down by the river just talking. Wanda was drinking a beer, while Abby, the mother-to-be, was sipping on sparkling water.

"I can't even imagine. I'd have burrowed under the covers and prayed the bed swallowed me whole," Abby said.

Wanda snorted. "That would be one way to go. I, however, jumped out of the bed and promptly fell flat on my face. Then I calmly walked into the bathroom, got dressed, and left with my head held high."

"Oh, Wanda," Abby said, giving her a sympathetic but amused look. "That's… awful and completely hilarious all at the same time."

"I know." Wanda let out a sigh. "Now I'm going to have to hide out until Cameron leaves town. How's your guest room?"

"Full of baby stuff." Abby placed her hands on her barely there baby bump. "Clay and I might be a little excited." Her eyes sparkled, and even under the moonlight it was impossible to miss the glow illuminating her skin.

Wanda loved seeing her best friend so happy. She and Clay were high school sweethearts, but they'd been separated for over ten years when they both left town soon after their friend Charlotte Pelsh passed away. Her death was tragic, and Abby especially hadn't handled it well. But once she and Clay both moved back to town, they'd managed to find their way back to each other. It hadn't been easy for either of them, but they were the most in-love couple Wanda had ever known. They were the perfect example of relationship goals. Except Wanda had never wanted to get married. She'd always been happy being single. And then Cameron Copeland came along.

The man just did things for her. He was sexy, fun, and easy going. And perfect for her. His job kept him traveling for work, which meant he had his life and she had hers. They got together when he was in town and when he was gone, she missed him sure, but she also relished her alone time and the fact that she never had to answer to anyone but herself.

Independence was Wanda's middle name.

"Can I throw you a baby shower, or do your sisters have that covered?" Wanda asked Abby. "You know how much I love a party."

Abby gave her friend a huge grin. "I would love that. I think Noel has her hands full with my precious baby niece, so I wouldn't worry about her having any plans for a shower. Check with Yvette and Faith though. They've been feeling me out on what kind of stuff we need, so they probably are up to something."

"On it." Wanda hadn't ever wanted any children of her own, but she sure did enjoy spoiling the Townsend sisters' little ones. She was happy playing the favorite aunt to the family that had always treated her as one of their own.

"I need ice cream," Abby said suddenly. "No. Scratch that. Put this golf cart in gear, and let's head to the brew pub. There's a warm brownie sundae on the menu that's calling my name."

"Beer and brownies? Now you're talking." Wanda did as her friend asked, and this time when she turned the music on, she chose “1999” by Prince. As the cart jerked forward, the song blared from the speakers while the flashing purple lights lit up the night.

“Whoo hoo!” Abby threw her arms in the air and started to sing along with the song at the top of her lungs.

Wanda glanced at her and felt the joy that bubbled up in her chest when she was with the people she loved. Earlier, when she’d fled from Cameron and his parents, she’d been humiliated and hurt when Cameron had introduced her as just a friend.

Just a friend.

What was that? Even though they hadn’t made any promises to each other and she wasn’t looking for a ring, she wasn’t in the habit of hooking up with just anyone. *Friends* wasn’t how she’d describe their relationship.

But she couldn’t help the nagging voice that asked, *What else was he supposed to say?* Girlfriend? The woman he was dating? Or more accurately, the woman he was sleeping with?

Wanda let out a disgusted grunt. Had she lost her mind?

“What was that about?” Abby asked. “Thinking about Cameron again?”

“Who else?” Wanda turned the golf cart onto Main Street and turned up the music so she wouldn’t have to verbalize her thoughts.

Abby seemed to get the message, because instead of probing, she once again started singing along with Prince at the top of her lungs.

Wanda felt her lips tug up into a tiny smile as she sent out a silent thanks for her bestie, Abby Townsend.

Five minutes later, they were sitting at a table at the Townsend brewpub. Wanda opted for one of their new hard apple ciders while Abby was drinking a new herbal tea she'd been responsible for getting on the menu.

"Tea and a brownie sundae?" Wanda asked with a laugh. "Seems an odd combo."

"My other option is hot chocolate, and that's too much chocolate even for me."

"Really? Since when?" Wanda eyed her friend and then the belly bump. "I've seen you eat an entire bag of snack-size Halloween candy and wash it down with a giant glass of chocolate milk."

Abby grimaced. Then she chuckled. "Can you believe it? I think this baby has a mind of her own. If she comes out with even a slight aversion to chocolate, I'm going to have to wonder what alien did this to me because no kid of mine could possibly have an anti-chocolate gene."

"Seems reasonable to me," Wanda said in support of her friend as she smiled at Rhys, the assistant manager of the brewpub.

He placed the oversized brownie sundaes in front of them and asked, "Anything else, ladies?"

"Hot chocolate." Wanda winked at Abby. "Two."

Abby groaned but didn't correct her friend.

Rhys laughed. "On it."

"You're the devil," Abby said and then shoved a giant spoonful of brownie and ice cream in her mouth.

Wanda was digging into her own sundae when her phone buzzed with a text. She almost ignored it, but she couldn't stop herself from wondering if Cameron was trying to get in touch with her. But when she glanced at the screen, the text was from a number she didn't recognize. She frowned and tapped the screen.

Wanda, it's Blake. Where are you?

"Blake?" Wanda whispered. She hadn't talked to her half sister in over nine months. Not since she and her father had a falling out and he told her he was done with her. Wanda had been relieved. Her relationship with her father had always been a tumultuous one, and the only reason she'd been in touch with him at all was because of her sister Blake. But when her dad cut her off, her communication with Blake had ended too. Fear curled in Wanda's gut. Why did her sister have a new number? She quickly tapped out a text letting her know she was at the pub. Then she added, *Why? Where are you?*

On your front porch.

Wanda didn't even bother to ask why her sister was in Keating Hollow. There was only one reason Blake would travel across the country unannounced. Something had happened with their father. *The key is under the pot with the painted sunflower. Go on in. I'll be right there.*

"What's wrong?" Abby asked, placing her spoon on the table and giving Wanda her full attention. "You look like you're ready to murder someone."

Wanda threw a couple of bills on the table and stood. "Not someone. My father. Sorry, Abs. I gotta go. Blake just showed up on my doorstep."

"Blake?" Abby's eyes widened. "How? Doesn't she live in North Carolina?"

"Yes, she does. And I don't know how she got here. A seventeen-year-old can't rent a car." Wanda's stomach rolled as she tried not to jump to conclusions. Blake was a smart girl. Surely she hadn't taken any unnecessary risks. "I'll call you later."

"Maybe you should take her your brownie. We can wrap it up really quick," Abby said.

Wanda shook her head. "You take it. I've got stuff in my freezer." Then without another word, she strode out of the brewery, completely forgetting that she'd been Abby's ride.

It didn't take long for Wanda to arrive at her two-story craftsman at the edge of town. The home was in the hills just below the mountain and had a gorgeous view of the town and the river. She'd purchased it a few years ago as a fixer-upper, and she'd spent countless hours refinishing her kitchen and bathroom cabinets, redoing the decks, and painting every room. It was her pride and joy and her sanctuary.

A small SUV was parked in her normally empty driveway, and she let out a sigh of relief. Her sister had managed to get her hands on a vehicle. Thank the gods. Wanda hit her garage door remote and pulled her golf cart inside. As she was climbing out of the cart, her sister ran into the garage, dropped a duffle bag, and nearly knocked Wanda over with her embrace.

"I missed you so much," Blake said, her voice breaking with emotion as she held on tight.

"I missed you, too, Blake." Wanda held onto her sister and ran a hand over her long dark hair. When she pulled back, there was no missing the tears streaming down the teenager's face. "What happened?"

"They just… left," she gasped out.

"What do you mean left?" Wanda frowned at the teen. "Who left?"

"Mom and Dad." More tears streamed down her face unchecked. "I came home from a weekend trip to the beach with friends, and most of their stuff was gone." She sucked in a shuddering breath. "Mom left a note with a prepaid credit card and told me they were going off grid."

"Off grid?" Wanda said lamely, trying and failing to comprehend what her sister was saying. Had they loaded up an RV and taken off for the desert or something? "What does that mean, exactly?"

Blake shook her head. "I don't know. Dad's been talking about backpacking around the world for the past few years. But lately they..." She swallowed hard. "Mom's been using again."

"And Dad?" Wanda asked, her heart nearly beating out of her chest. Her dad had left her and her mom when Wanda was little. He'd been a functioning alcoholic. Years later when he finally reached out, he'd told her he was sober. She was happy of course, but their relationship had never recovered. As for Blake, she'd been with her grandparents off and on, but once her dad got sober, she'd moved in with her parents permanently. Now Wanda was wondering just how bad it had gotten if they'd just up and left her.

She shrugged. "I don't know. He hides it well."

There were so many questions that Wanda wanted to ask her, but there would be time for that later. "Okay. Let's go in and I'll make hot chocolate and get you something to eat. Then we'll talk more."

Blake nodded but stared at her feet. Her hands were trembling, and Wanda couldn't imagine how scared she must be.

"Blake?"

"Yeah?" She glanced up and blinked away the tears still pooled in her eyes.

"You're safe, sweetie. My home is yours. I promise. No matter what, I'm here for you. Understand?"

Blake nodded again but clutched her bag tighter.

"Come on." Wanda opened the door in the garage that led

to her kitchen. "You go on upstairs and drop your stuff in the guest room. First one on the right at the top of the stairs. I'll get the hot cocoa going. Okay?"

"Do you have marshmallows?" Blake asked with a fragile smile.

Wanda grinned. "What kind of question is that? Of course I do. Hurry up or else I'll eat them all." Wanda winked at her, remembering the one time her father had brought Blake to Keating Hollow about seven years ago. It had been summertime, and Wanda had spent the entire week trying to win her little sister over with every treat in the book. The toasted marshmallows had finally done the trick.

Blake turned around and started toward the living area. But then she stopped and glanced over her shoulder. In a very tiny voice, she said, "Thank you, Wanda."

Wanda's heart nearly broke at what her parents had done to her. She wanted to wrap her arms around the young woman and physically hold her together so that she didn't come apart at the seams. Because it was all too clear now that she was safe, it was likely the young woman would finally succumb to a meltdown. "Ah, baby. There's nothing to thank me for. This is what family is supposed to do."

The tears were back in her eyes, but this time when Blake turned around, the tension that had been holding her shoulders so rigid seemed to ease a bit. And Wanda wondered how long it would be before she saw the happy, bubbly girl she'd first met seven years ago.

CHAPTER 2

"Cameron," Emily Copeland said in her mom voice. She was standing in the doorway of one of their rooms at the Keating Hollow Inn. He'd been surprised when his parents decided last minute to tag along to visit the magical village, but not nearly as surprised as when they'd walked in on Wanda, who'd been waiting for him in one of their rooms almost naked. "You chase after that girl right this minute. This is not the time to let things go."

"She's not a girl, Mom," he said, revisiting the image of Wanda in her sexy see-through outfit. He nearly let out a groan at the memory of her lush curves. But when his mother spoke again, all thoughts of the lovely woman fled, and his cheeks heated with embarrassment. Why did he have to be talking to his mother about this?

"It takes a lot of nerve, not to mention trust, to surprise a man like that," she said, one hand raised as she pointed at him. "I'm telling you, if you don't do something to smooth this over, it won't be happening again. If you want to keep a woman like that happy, you'll go find her and make sure she knows you appreciate her efforts."

Cameron groaned. It wasn't that he didn't want to run to Wanda's house. Every cell inside of him was screaming for him to do just that. But he felt strange and awkward now that his parents were trying to urge him on. "Please stop. This isn't helping."

"She's right, son," his father said from behind her. Dayton Copeland towered over his wife and winked at his son as he added, "Go find that girl and finish what she started."

"Enough." Cameron walked over to the door, gently pushing them both back into the hall. "This conversation is over. I'll see you both in the morning for breakfast."

"Not too early," Dayton called. "We wouldn't want you to rush back from your girlfriend's house."

Cameron shut the door without responding. Wanda wasn't his girlfriend. Or was she? No. They hadn't had that conversation. In fact, they'd both been careful to not define their relationship at all. What they had was a couple of weeks of really good sex and a lot of laughs. The only promise he'd made was that he'd be back. And she hadn't made any at all.

Still, he hadn't missed her obvious annoyance when he'd said she was a friend. He let out another groan. There was no denying that his parents were right. He should go to her. He was only in town for a few days before he had to get back to set, so what was he doing wasting time? Without another thought, he grabbed his small carryon bag and the key to his rental car and strode out of his room.

"Oh, good," his mother said, startling him. She was standing at her door with a ceramic mug in her hand. She must've ventured downstairs to the coffee and tea bar that

Noel kept in the lobby. "Have fun. Don't forget to be safe. Remember, no glove, no love."

Cameron just shook his head and pretended that his face wasn't burning with embarrassment. "See you in the morning, Mother."

"*Mother.*" She let out a snort and pushed her door open. Just before it closed, he heard her add, "He's such an easy mark."

Cameron couldn't help it. He chuckled. She'd been needling him on purpose, and that was just one of the reasons he loved her so much. He knew he was lucky. His parents had always been laid back, fun, and his biggest supporters. He just wished they wouldn't share every thought that ran through their heads. Sometimes boundaries were a good thing.

Wanda's craftsman home was dark when he pulled his rental into the driveway. It was getting late, and he wondered if she'd already gone to bed. Though that wasn't like her. Wanda was a night owl, just like he was. After his knock on the door went unanswered, he decided to take a page out of Wanda's book and retrieved the key from under the sunflower pot. Once he was inside, he called her name. If she was home, he didn't want to startle her. When she didn't respond, he smiled to himself and made his way upstairs.

It wasn't the first time he'd been in her house, and he headed straight for her bedroom. He glanced at the perfectly made bed and couldn't wait to mess it up with her. Smiling to himself, he moved to the fireplace and touched the wicks of the candles lined up on her mantle. They instantly came to life with flickering flames. Then he touched the painting of the redwood forest, bringing the babbling brook to life and intensifying the light shining through the trees.

Being a spirit witch, he had unique and unusual abilities. All spirit witches did, and almost none of them shared the same abilities. Cameron learned when he was a young boy that he had the ability to manipulate multiple elements. His precociousness had all but driven his mother crazy, like when he changed the fruit into cookies. They never tasted as good as the real thing, but they were better than the overripe bananas his mother favored.

After touching another painting, this one a garden of roses, Cameron directed the rose petals to make their way to the bed. The entire scene was straight out of a rom-com, and likely Wanda would tease him relentlessly, but he knew she'd appreciate the gesture all the same. With the bedroom mood set, Cameron headed across the hall to the oversized bathroom to shuck his clothes. Not wanting to just sit on the bed naked like some sort of porn star, he wrapped one of her plush white towels around his waist and intended to head back to the bedroom.

But as soon as Cameron opened the door, he ran right into a tall teenager who shrieked and jerked back, her hands up as if she were ready to fight him.

"Whoa!" Cameron said, startled. He had a short moment of panic where he wondered if he'd broken into the wrong house. What was a strange teenager doing there? But he instantly dismissed the thought. Of course this was Wanda's house. He wasn't that far gone that he didn't recognize her home.

"Who the hell are you?" the teenager demanded. "Are you Wanda's boyfriend or something?"

"Um, something like that," he said, glancing over his shoulder at the bathroom where his clothes were folded in a pile. He took a step back while clutching at the towel to keep it from falling. "I should—"

"What's wrong?" Wanda's voice carried up from the stairs.

Cameron heard her footsteps just before she rounded the corner and came to an abrupt halt.

"Cam? What's going on?" She glanced at the teenager and then back to Cameron.

"I came over to talk to you, and when I realized you weren't home, I thought I'd surprise you, like you tried to do for me earlier. I didn't expect our experiences to be quite so similar," he said as he tilted his head toward the younger woman.

Wanda blinked. Then she let out a loud bark of laughter. After wiping the tears of amusement from her eyes, she waved at the girl standing beside her. "Cameron, this is my sister, Blake. Blake, this is my *friend,* Cameron."

"Friend, huh?" Blake said, raising one eyebrow exactly the same way Wanda did when she knew she was being fed a load of crap. "I don't recall any of my friends surprising me in nothing but a towel, but if that's what you want to call it, then okay." She smoothed her long hair back, nodded to the bathroom, and added, "If you'll excuse me, I need to use the facilities."

"Right." Cameron stepped out of the way and watched as Blake disappeared into the bathroom where his clothes were still folded neatly on the vanity.

Wanda grinned up at Cameron and shook her head. "So... What brings you here this evening?"

Cameron glanced down at his towel and then back at Wanda with a pointed look. "I thought that was obvious."

"Yeah. I guess it is." She took a step closer and whispered

in his ear. "Why don't you put some clothes on and meet me downstairs?"

"I would, but they're in there." He pointed to the bathroom.

Wanda let out another small bark of laughter. "Of course they are." Then she shoved him into her bedroom, but instead of following him, she stood in the doorway and said, "Stay here until my sister is done. Then get dressed and meet me downstairs."

Before Cameron could say another word, she gave him a smirk and closed the door, leaving him alone in her bedroom. Cameron let out a small laugh and decided right then and there that Wanda Danvers just might be the most perfect woman he'd ever met.

He listened to her footsteps as she made her way down the stairs then turned to look at the spectacle he'd created in her room and shook his head. It was a damned shame all that romance was going to waste. "Better luck next time, man," he mumbled to himself.

After he heard a second set of steps on the stairs, he ventured out into the hall and back into the bathroom. A few minutes later, he found Wanda in her kitchen, bustling about, making a fresh pot of coffee.

"Where's your sister?" he asked, leaning against the doorframe.

Wanda shrugged and gave him a faint smile. "Anywhere but here. I think finding a naked man in a towel might have been a little more excitement than she bargained for."

"She's not the only one who got more than they bargained for this evening," Cameron said, joining her in the kitchen and taking one of the mugs from her.

"Nope, she isn't." Wanda walked over to the breakfast

table that was in an alcove framed by a bay window. She took a seat and smiled up at him. "Are your parents scarred for life?"

Cameron chuckled, remembering his mother ordering him to pursue Wanda after she'd rushed out of the inn. "You'll soon find out that my mother has very few boundaries. Walking in on a lover waiting for her son is never going to faze her."

"Lover? I guess that's more accurate than *friend,*" Wanda said.

Cameron didn't miss the sarcasm in her tone. He gazed at her, studying her carefully blank expression. "It is, but it's not exactly something I wanted to announce to my mother."

"I think she already knew, Cam," Wanda said softly as her cheeks flushed pink.

Damn, she was sexy like that. Wanda wasn't one to embarrass easily. She was full of confidence and lived her life unapologetically. Those qualities were why he liked her so much. But he had to admit that seeing her flush because she'd been waiting for him practically naked made his insides flutter. "Sure, but she didn't need confirmation from me. Some things are meant to be kept private."

Her lips twitched slightly as she shook her head. "You do realize that the entire town knows we have a thing, right?"

"Do they?" he asked innocently. Of course he knew that. Keating Hollow was a small town, and the residents lived for gossip. Even if Wanda hadn't told anyone, everyone saw them leave the Christmas ball together, and more than one person had noticed Wanda leaving the inn in her ball gown the next morning after they'd spent the night in his room. Not to mention they hadn't exactly been hiding in his room.

They'd eaten out plenty of times at the various restaurants and cafés.

She raised one eyebrow and stared him down.

Cameron chuckled. "Okay, you're right. They do. I'm still not discussing any of this with my mother."

"Fair enough." She turned her attention to her coffee mug.

"Listen," he said, hesitatingly. "I'm sorry about referring to our relationship as just friends. It doesn't take a genius to realize you didn't appreciate that characterization."

Wanda blew out a breath. "No. I'm sorry. Obviously I misread things. It's not like we discussed the status of our relationship."

He reached out and placed a hand over hers. "It's no secret that I like you, Wanda."

"I like you, too," she said, her eyes glinting in the soft lighting.

"That's good to hear. I wouldn't be excited to find out you didn't." He winked at her. "Now that we have that out of the way, what do you say? Should I refer to you as my girlfriend?"

Just as she started to open her mouth, the tall teenager strode in. She waved her hands in the air and said, "Don't mind me. I just came in to get something to drink and a snack. I'll be out of your hair in a minute."

Cameron didn't say anything as he watched her rummage in the fridge for a soda and then grab a bag of pretzels from the pantry.

Once Blake disappeared into another part of the house, Cameron peered at Wanda. "So…"

"So…" she echoed and then sighed. "Listen, Cam. I know I

was put out earlier when you called me your friend, but the truth is that's what we are, right?"

"Yes, but—"

She held her hand up, stopping him.

He desperately wanted to restart the evening. Ditch his parents and book them a short-term rental or put them up in Eureka, anywhere but the Keating Hollow Inn where they'd walked in on Wanda. Because this was starting to look like Wanda was slamming on the brakes. And that was the last thing he wanted.

"I'm sorry. Tonight has been strange. First your parents and now my little sister is here out of the blue. Do you think we could talk about this another time?"

Cameron searched her expression. She was doing her best to hide her stress, but there was no mistaking the tension in her raised shoulders or the way she kept stretching her neck as if she had a kink. Both were uncharacteristic of the woman sitting across from him. "Of course. I'm sorry to barge in," he said as he stood. "I just wanted you to know how much I appreciated finding you in what was supposed to be *my* room. If things hadn't gone south on us, I'd have enjoyed every moment of our night together."

"Me, too." Wanda stood and moved over to link her arm through his. "But for now, I need to talk to my sister. Can I call you tomorrow?"

"I'm counting on it." He pressed a soft kiss to her cheek and opened the front door.

Wanda followed him out, and the moment they were on the porch, she closed the door and then pressed him up against the porch railing, bringing her lips within an inch of his.

Cameron's breath hitched as his body instantly responded to her. "This isn't how I usually say goodnight to my friends," he teased.

Her eyes glittered in the moonlight. "Me neither." Then she pressed her lips to his and kissed him with everything she had.

CHAPTER 3

Wanda's lips were still tingling when she walked back into her house. It had taken every ounce of willpower to send Cameron away, to not claim him as her boyfriend when he'd asked her to define what they were to each other. Gods, she'd wanted to, and that, more than anything, had scared the ever-loving crap out of her. Wanda wasn't one to dive into relationships, especially after only a few weeks, most of which they'd been in separate towns. It was too soon, and she had her sister to worry about.

"I'm surprised you didn't just haul your *friend* into your bedroom and have your naughty way with him," Blake said from where she was curled up in an oversized chair in the corner of the living room.

Wanda jumped as her heart nearly leaped right out of her chest. "Holy crap, Blake. You scared the hell out of me."

Her sister chuckled. "Sorry. I thought you saw me when you dragged that hot man out of here."

Wanda walked over to the end of her couch and sat down. “Hand me some pretzels.”

Blake passed the bag to Wanda and said, “I’m done with them.”

“Thanks.” Wanda ate a couple of pretzels and then studied her sister, narrowing her eyes as she realized the car in the driveway had belonged to Cameron, not Blake. “How did you get here?”

Blake averted her gaze and studied a painting of the village that hung on Wanda’s wall.

After a moment of complete silence, Wanda cleared her throat. “Blake? Answer me. How did you get to California?”

“I bought a bus ticket.”

“The bus!” Wanda sat up straight, her entire body rigid. “You took a bus from North Carolina all the way to Eureka? How many days was that?”

“Four,” she whispered.

“Four days!” Wanda’s blood pressure skyrocketed as a variety of terrifying thoughts flashed through her mind. Her beautiful young sister just spent four days on a bus, traveling across country. No one knew where she was, and anything could have happened to her. “Why didn’t you just call me? I’d have gotten you an airline ticket.”

“I didn’t have your number,” she said, suddenly sounding exhausted. “I got it from the woman at the inn. I stopped there, thinking I’d get a room if I had to, but Noel said she knew you and gave me your number after she forced me to eat a sandwich.”

Wanda wanted to kiss Noel for taking care of her sister. “Do I even want to know how you got here from Eureka?” The bus didn’t travel between the two towns. The only options were personal vehicles and taxis.

"No." Blake's lips formed a large *O* as she yawned. After she wiped at her tearing eyes, she added, "Don't worry, I made sure to scan her energy before I got into her car."

"You hitchhiked?" Wanda was ready to jump right out of her skin. "Are you insane?"

"No," she said with a dismissive wave of her hand. "I asked around the bus station if anyone was headed to Keating Hollow, and if so, if I could get a ride. A woman named Hope had just dropped off her brother and said I could ride with her. If she'd been a serial killer, I'd have probably caught on."

"Hope Garber? Blond hair, early twenties?" Wanda asked, already feeling the tension drain from her limbs. Hope was Abby Townsend's half sister. If Blake rode with her, she'd been perfectly safe. Thank the gods.

"Yep. That's her. She was sweet and wouldn't even let me give her gas money."

"That sounds like Hope." Wanda made a mental note to make the woman a basket of homemade cookies as a thank you for taking care of Blake. She didn't even want to think about what could've happened to her sister if some other stranger had offered her a ride. Of course Blake's magical ability did give her quite the advantage.

Wanda eyed her sister thoughtfully. Because Wanda hadn't spent a lot of time with Blake over the years, she often forgot about her spirit witch ability that let her read a person's energy, or what was also referred to as a person's aura. She could get a feel for their overall state of being. If they were sad, happy, cagey, void of emotion. That kind of thing. It served her well in reading people. Being a spirit witch was something Blake had in common with Cameron. Wanda was often wowed by their unique abilities.

Meanwhile, Wanda was a fire witch and all she could really do was manipulate that element. It was helpful in the winter when she wanted a never-ending fire, but overall, she didn't exactly use her gift that much on a regular basis. What did she need fire for as a real estate agent?

Blake clutched her soda can and kept her eyes averted as if she was hoping she'd just disappear right into thin air to avoid the coming conversation.

Wanda wasn't having that. There was no better way to start a conversation than to just get right to the point. She took a deep breath and said, "I think you'd better tell me what's going on."

"What's there to tell? The parentals bailed, so I did, too." Blake's tone was flippant as if she didn't care that her parents were gone. But Wanda wasn't fooled. Her sister's eyes were almost haunted, and her face was pinched with tension.

"Come on, sis. How long have they been using? Did the note say anything about when they'd be back? And what about your grandparents? Do they know what's going on?"

"No, no, and no." Blake placed her hand over her eyes, and a moment later she let out a tiny sob.

Son of a... Wanda cursed herself. She shouldn't have been pushing Blake so hard to answer her questions. The girl had just spent four days traveling on a bus after finding out her parents had just up and left her to fend for herself. What Blake needed was somewhere safe to rest, some food, and someone to hold onto her, to make sure she knew she was safe. Wanda pushed herself off the couch and went to kneel in front of her sister. "Hey," she said softly. "You know I'm here for you. Whatever you need, right?"

Blake nodded, but didn't remove her hand.

"No matter what," Wanda added, wanting desperately to

pull the young woman into her arms and hold her. But from the way Blake was curling into herself, it was clear she was completely closed off, and Wanda wasn't going to force herself on her. "My spare bedroom is yours as long as you want it." Hell, as far as Wanda was concerned, Blake was never going to leave. Not if she had anything to say about it. Her parents were in no way equipped to have custody of Blake, even if she was seventeen and almost an adult. Her sister needed someone in her corner, and Wanda was determined to be that person. She just couldn't sit by and let her get hurt again.

"Thank you," Blake forced out. She sucked in a shuddering breath, removed her hands from her eyes, and met Wanda's gaze with a determined expression. "As soon as we talk to Grandma, I'm sure she'll send me an airline ticket and I'll be out of your hair."

"You didn't call her already?" Wanda frowned, wondering belatedly why Blake hadn't gotten in touch with her mother's parents. They were the ones who'd had custody of her before her parents had gotten clean. No doubt they'd have done whatever was necessary to get her to Maine where they lived.

Tears filled Blake's eyes, but she quickly wiped them away as she cleared her throat. "Grandpa passed on six months ago. Heart attack."

"Oh, no, Blake. I'm so sorry, honey," Wanda said. "I didn't know."

"I guess you wouldn't have." She glanced out the window again. "Grandma moved to be closer to my aunt in Vermont after that, and I don't have their numbers. Grandma's old one is disconnected. So I came here. I'm sure once we track down Grandma, I can get out of your hair."

Wanda's heart nearly broke for her sister. She knew what it meant to be abandoned and then eventually alone. Her father had abandoned her when she was young, and then after her mother died, Wanda didn't have anyone. Well, no one but the Townsends. Lincoln Townsend, Abby's father, had always been there for her, but she hadn't had any family of her own she could rely on. The only difference between Wanda and Blake was that Wanda was already out of college when her mom died. She hadn't been a teenager still trying to figure out how she was going to survive.

"Blake, you're not in my way," Wanda said, staring her sister in the eye. "You are welcome here always, for however long you want to be here. Okay?"

"Yeah, sure," she said quietly as she glanced away. Then another yawn overtook her, and she covered her mouth. "Sorry. It's been a week."

Wanda walked over to her, tugged her to her feet, and then wrapped her in a giant hug, holding on as if she were literally trying to hold the girl together. "I'm glad you're here and that you're safe. And I'm so sorry for what Dad and your mom did. You deserve better."

Blake clung to her, and her body shook slightly.

Wanda squeezed her eyes shut, trying not to cry. "I love you, and I want you to always remember that no matter what they did, you are *not* disposable. Understand?"

Her sister nodded even as she kept her head buried in Wanda's shoulder.

The pair stood together, arms wrapped around each other for a long time, until finally, Blake pulled back and said, "Thank you."

"Nothing to thank me for. We're family." She smiled at

her. "Now come on. Let's get some sleep. Things will look better in the morning."

"Yeah. Okay." Blake shuffled toward the stairs.

Wanda followed, her heart heavy with what Blake's parents had done. But as she watched her sister move through her house, she vowed that, no matter what, Blake would never be alone again. Not if Wanda had anything to say about it.

CHAPTER 4

"Cameron Copeland!" his mother admonished incredulously as she emerged into the lobby of the Keating Hollow Inn. She placed her hands on her hips and eyed him while he poured himself a cup of coffee from the complimentary breakfast bar. "What are you doing back here so early? Do not tell me you got up in the middle of the night and left that lovely woman alone in her bed. You should be over there making her breakfast and treating her like a goddess." She *tsked*. "Have I taught you nothing?"

Noel Townsend, who had a baby tucked against her shoulder, snickered from her place behind the check-in counter.

Cameron's face heated, and he cleared his throat. "I don't think this is an appropriate discussion to have with my mother."

"The heck it's not. No son of mine is going to treat any woman as if she's just a booty call." Emily Copeland leveled him with a stare that practically dared him to argue with her.

Knowing he'd never win the argument, Cameron gave up

on the idea that he'd be able to maintain any kind of privacy and said, "If you must know, I did go see Wanda but for only a few minutes. Her sister arrived unexpectedly, and I wasn't invited to stay."

"Oh. I see." His mother's expression turned to one of amused sympathy. "I am sorry to hear that. Sounds like the two of you have terrible timing."

"You can say that again." Cameron shrugged, wanting to sidestep any discussion of his non-existent sex life.

"Are you talking about Blake?" Noel asked.

"Yes, that's Wanda's sister. Why? Did something happen?" Cameron asked, wondering if there'd been some sort of trouble overnight. He'd wanted to call Wanda that morning but refrained so he wouldn't be that needy guy when she was dealing with family stuff.

"No. Not really," Noel said, frowning. "Hope dropped her off here after giving her a ride to Keating Hollow from the bus station in Eureka. I gave her something to eat and Wanda's number and address after she said she was looking for her. She looked tired and a little scared, but definitely wasn't interested in sharing any details about where she'd come from or how she'd gotten here. I was just worried about her and hoping everything is okay."

"Damn. That doesn't sound good." Cameron muttered, feeling his face heat. Wanda had told him that her sister had arrived unexpectedly, but he hadn't realized there might be something wrong. Blake had seemed all right when she caught him in a towel, but maybe that was just the distraction she needed to get her mind off her troubles. Regardless, Cameron felt like an ass for barging in on what might have been a family emergency. There was no question; he'd need to swallow his pride later and give

Wanda a call to make sure she and her sister were doing okay.

"Whatever it is, Wanda will take care of her," Noel said with total confidence.

Cameron nodded. There was no doubt about that. Cameron hadn't ever met a woman with a bigger heart. He turned to his mother. "I need to meet Miranda for a business meeting this morning. Can you and dad meet me for lunch at the Townsend Brewery?"

"Sure, honey. Your father and I are going to stroll this lovely town for a while, and we can meet you there about one. Does that work?"

He nodded and leaned in to give her a kiss on the cheek. "Have fun."

"Oh, wait, dear." His mother wrapped her small hand around his wrist, stopping him. "After all of the excitement last night, I forgot to tell you I got a call from a young man who said he's Victoria's son. He wanted to get in touch with you."

"Victoria?" Cameron racked his brain, trying to place who that might be, but he came up blank. "I don't know anyone by that name."

"Of course you do, Cam," his mother said, slightly exasperated. "Victoria. That sweet girl you dated your freshmen year in college."

"Tori?" Cameron frowned as an old familiar dull ache reappeared in his chest. Tori had been his first love. The one who'd broken his heart when she left him a dear John letter and disappeared from his life. He'd been so in love with her, and the next thing he knew, she was gone with no explanation, just a hastily written apology and a plea for him to not hate her. It hadn't worked. After he'd gotten over the devastation, anger had filled all the cracked spaces in his heart. He'd been a mess for a long time. Then he'd put the relationship behind him and vowed to always keep it casual. And that's what he'd done for the past twenty years. "She has a son?"

"It appears so," she said.

"What does he want with me?"

"I don't know, honey." She pulled one of her own business cards out of her purse and handed it to him. "His number is on the back. Why don't you give him a call and find out?"

That wasn't likely. Cameron could only think of one reason why some kid he'd never met would be calling him—his Hollywood connections. Cameron was a well-known screenwriter who was working on two high profile projects. Not only did he not have time to mentor someone, he'd learned the hard way that most people asking for help were nowhere near ready for prime time. Tori's son would just have to pay his dues in the industry like everyone else. Still, he took the card to appease his mother and mumbled something about maybe calling later.

His mother leveled him with a knowing stare. "You're not going to call him back, are you?"

Cameron shrugged and then changed the subject. "I've got to go. See you and dad for lunch."

He heard his mother let out a sigh just before he disappeared out onto Main Street.

"Cameron!" Miranda Moon called as she strutted down the cobbled streets in her silver corset dress and thigh-high black boots.

"Hey, partner," Cameron said, picking up his pace to meet her. After a quick hug, he held the beautiful brunette away from him and scanned her outfit. "What's with the tiny velvet bows? This look is a little sweet for you, isn't it?"

Miranda ran a finger over the delicate black trim and blushed. Actually blushed. "It's romantic," Miranda said, her lips curving into a shy smile. "I guess I've softened a little and stepped away from my all-black persona."

Cameron snorted. "No kidding. Looks like Gideon has smoothed your edges."

"He does more than that," she said with a sly smile. "But that's a conversation for another time. Ready to get to work?"

"You have no idea."

THE SCENT of rich coffee filled the air as Cameron's fingers flew over the keyboard. Miranda sat across from him, reading off the revisions they'd made to the script they'd sold a few months ago. The network had come back with notes and had asked for changes before they started filming.

When the last of the changes were made, Cameron sat back in his chair and let out a sigh of relief. He'd been afraid they'd end up spending days working on the project. Instead, they worked so well together that they'd done it in a matter of a few hours. "You're incredible, Miranda."

The novelist sitting across from him tilted her head to the side, and her lips twitched into a small smile. "Cam, is this your way of trying to woo me away from Gideon?"

He chuckled. "Not unless he's become your new writing partner."

She laughed. "Hardly. He's too busy hiding away in his

new studio working on goddess knows what. He's been sculpting something, but he's being tight-lipped about it."

"I'm guessing he's the type of artist who doesn't like input on his work while it's in progress," Cameron said, completely understanding that process. He was exactly the same way with his writing, except when he was working with Miranda. They just had a rare magical connection.

"It appears so." She winked. "I suppose we're all just a bunch of temperamental artists."

Cameron was still smiling as the pair of them left the Incantation Café a few moments later and headed for the Keating Hollow Brewery. "Are you sure you're up for this?" he asked Miranda after they were seated.

"Up for what? Meeting your parents?" She ordered a pear cider from the waitress and scanned the menu.

"Yeah. I'm warning you now, my mom will find a way to get you to spill all of my secrets without you even realizing it," Cameron said, already feeling the need to bolt. Even though Miranda was nothing more than a friend and co-writer, he knew that wouldn't stop his mother from grilling her. Emily Copeland had a reputation for slyly prying details about his life out of anyone who would speak to her. She'd likely have Miranda relaying his entire history of his time in Keating Hollow before the lunch was over. It was just in her DNA. He loved his mother, but he wasn't looking forward to the inquisition, no matter how benign it seemed.

"But I don't know your secrets," Miranda said with a laugh. "What does she think she'll get? How long it takes you to write a page of dialog?"

"You're laughing now, but you just wait."

CHAPTER 5

Wanda gently laid her phone down on the counter and pressed her fingertips to her temple. The headache had set in about two minutes into the phone call with Blake's aunt. The nausea had started as soon as the woman had made it clear why Blake would not be moving to Vermont to be with her grandmother.

"Was that her?" Blake asked excitedly as she hurried into the kitchen. She'd pulled her dark hair into a high ponytail and was wearing a pink tank top with matching flannel pajama bottoms. Her freshly washed face was full of hope, making her look even younger than her seventeen years.

It hadn't taken Wanda long to track down her Aunt Linda. She'd run a property search for Linda DeWitt and the address had come right up. Once she had the address, finding a phone number hadn't been an issue. The trouble had come after Linda nearly bit her head off for suggesting she let Blake talk to her grandmother.

"That was your aunt Linda," Wanda said, trying to keep

her tone neutral. "She wanted me to tell you how sorry she is that your mom has relapsed."

Blake's innocent expression hardened, and her eyes flashed with anger. "Linda's always sorry, but that doesn't mean she wants me to move back in with Grandma. What did Grandma say? Did you talk to her?"

Wanda shook her head while she took a moment to digest Blake's revelation. "Since when does your aunt have a problem with you living with your grandmother?"

"Since always," Blake said with a sigh. "She was forever telling Grandma it wasn't her job to raise me. I think she hates me and my mom."

"I'm sure she doesn't hate you," Wanda said, trying to calm her sister, even though she knew it was no use. Once she learned the status of the situation in Vermont, she was going to be crushed.

"Oh, she does." There was conviction in Blake's tone, and Wanda quickly realized she needed to stop trying to be the peacekeeper. Her sister obviously had a rocky history with her aunt. Wanda wouldn't be doing her any favors by pretending everything was just fine. "Never mind Aunt Linda. Did you talk to Grandma? Is she sending a plane ticket?"

Wanda was ready for the floor to open up and swallow her whole. The last thing she wanted to do was deliver more bad news. Blake had been through too much already. But she had no choice. She took a deep breath. "No, I didn't talk to her. Your grandmother was busy with a doctor's appointment. We'll try to get her on the phone later."

"Oh." Blake's shoulders slumped, but she jerked her head up almost immediately. "Is she all right? Why is she at the doctor?"

It was the moment of truth. Wanda grabbed the coffee pot and poured two cups. With them both in her hands, she gestured to the table, inviting Blake to join her.

"Something's really wrong, isn't it?" Blake asked, her voice shaking.

Wanda sat down and patted the seat next to her, but Blake froze. Her right hand clutched the top of the chair so hard that her knuckles turned white.

"Wanda. Tell me."

"It isn't as bad as it sounds." Wanda reached out and grabbed Blake's free hand, holding it tightly in hers.

The color drained from Blake's face, but her dark eyes held Wanda's gaze with an intensity that unnerved Wanda. That was a look from a young woman who'd experienced far too much pain in her short life. "Just say it."

"I don't think you're going to be able to go live with your grandma, Blake," Wanda said gently.

Blake stood stock-still for a moment and then sank into the chair. "Because of Aunt Linda or is Grandma sick?"

"Both." There was no point beating around the bush now. "Your grandma is living with Linda now, and there isn't a spare room."

"Living with her?" Blake parroted and then bit down on her bottom lip. Her eyes filled with tears, but she blinked them back. "She'd never do that unless she had to. Grandma is fiercely independent."

"You're right. I'm sorry, sweetie, but your grandmother has the beginning stages of dementia. Your aunt convinced her to move in so she could keep an eye on her."

Blake stared at Wanda for a long moment. Then she suddenly stood and hurried into the kitchen. She stood in front of the refrigerator, her hand on the handle, but she didn't open it.

Wanda's heart cracked in two. Her sister had no one. Everyone who was supposed to love her had left her in one way or another, and now she had to process the news that the one person who'd always been there for her was deteriorating.

It didn't take long before Blake's shoulders started to shake, and she stifled a sob.

Without a second thought, Wanda got to her feet, rushed over to Blake, and wrapped her arms around her from behind. She moved her lips close to her sister's ear and whispered, "You're okay, sweetie. I'm here. You're safe. Always. Got it?"

Blake shook her head and wiped frantically at her eyes as she forced out, "I need to talk to Grandma. She'll know what to do."

"Of course," Wanda agreed. "We'll try again this afternoon. But you know that no matter what happens you have a home here with me, right?"

Blake choked back another sob as she said, "I can't do that to you."

"You're not doing anything to me, little sis," Wanda said earnestly. Every fiber of her being wanted to take away Blake's pain so that she wouldn't have to continue to suffer. Unfortunately, she didn't have that power. Instead, she added, "If you stay, you're allowing me to love you. And that's an honor I don't take lightly. Understand?"

It took a few beats, but Blake did eventually nod her head. Then she placed her hands on top of Wanda's and gingerly extracted herself from Wanda's embrace. She moved silently toward the stairs, but just before she disappeared to the second floor, she finally looked at Wanda through puffy eyes. "Thank you."

"There's no need to thank me, but even so, you're very welcome."

Blake squeezed her eyes shut, nodded, and then continued up the stairs.

"WHERE DO YOU WANT TO EAT?" Wanda asked, forcing cheer into her voice. They were in Wanda's golf cart at the end of Main Street, discussing their options. It had taken a monumental effort, but after Blake spent most of the morning hiding in her room, Wanda had finally convinced her to go out for lunch. She wanted her sister to feel comfortable in her town, and the sooner she got out of the house the easier it would be to fall in love with Keating Hollow. Wanda knew that nothing was going to replace the security that Blake felt living with her grandmother, but she was determined to do everything she could to help her sister settle in. Because there was no question about it—Blake was there to stay if Wanda had anything to say on the subject.

"It doesn't matter," Blake said, staring down the street but clearly not focusing on anything in particular.

Okay, so settling into Keating Hollow wasn't going to be fast or easy, but they had to start somewhere, right? "Are burgers okay?"

"Do they have veggie burgers?"

Finally, a spark of something other than indifference. "Yep. Black bean. Does that work?"

She nodded, and Wanda pressed down on the gas, making the golf cart shoot forward.

"Do you always drive this thing?" Blake asked her.

Wanda grinned. "If the weather's good, yes. And even sometimes when it isn't." She glanced over and winked at her sister. "My fire magic comes in handy when I need to keep warm."

Blake furrowed her eyebrows. "But why? Don't you have a perfectly good car?"

"Sure. But this is a hundred times more fun." To prove her point, Wanda flipped a switch and Miley Cyrus started belting out "Party in the USA" over the surround sound speakers.

"*This* is what you listen to?" Blake asked as if Wanda had committed a cardinal sin.

"Sure. It's fun," Wanda said, completely undeterred by her sister's obvious disapproval.

"I can't. You have to choose something else."

The conviction in her voice was such a welcome change from the indifference that Wanda merely nodded and hit a button. "Shake it Off" by Taylor Swift came on, causing Wanda to bounce in her seat.

"No!" Blake placed her hands over her ears and started to laugh. "Save me from bubblegum pop. Give me anything else. Anything at all."

"Anything?" Wanda snickered and hit the button again. This time Shania Twain came on singing about feeling like a woman.

"You can't be serious," Blake said, shaking her head. "Don't you have anything from this decade on there?" Laughing, she grabbed the remote and started hitting buttons until finally Prince came on. She sang "Purple Rain" at the top of her lungs, only stopping when Wanda pulled into a spot in front of the Keating Hollow Brewery.

"I thought you wanted something from this decade," Wanda said, her heart full after seeing the grin on her sister's face. A deep sense of satisfaction washed over her. It wasn't the first time a golf cart ride and Prince had lifted someone's spirits.

"Prince is timeless," Blake declared and hopped out of the cart. "Now hurry up. Suddenly I'm starving."

Wanda pocketed the golf cart key and followed her sister up the walk and through the front door of the brew pub.

"Hey, Wanda. Two for lunch?" asked Sadie, a petite blonde who'd been working at the pub for years.

"Yep. Sadie, this is my little sister, Blake. Blake, this is Sadie."

"Nice to meet you," Blake said, nodding at her.

"Oh, little sister," Sadie said, her eyes twinkling as if Wanda had just dropped the juiciest piece of gossip since the Hollywood star Silas Ansell had shown up in town. "You know, you two don't really look anything alike. Are you sure you're related?" Before Wanda could answer, Sadie eyed Blake and added, "But you do look a little like Brinn. Is she meeting you here? Do you need a table for three?"

Brinn? Blake mouthed to Wanda, clearly having no idea who Sadie was talking about. And why would she? Their father hadn't exactly made sure Blake met any of his extended family.

Wanda waved a carefree hand. "Not today. I'm pretty sure our cousin is working all day at the bookstore. We'll go by and say hi afterward."

"Got it." Sadie turned and gestured for them to follow.

"I have a cousin?" Blake whispered.

"Yep. She's really cool, too. You'll like her," Wanda whispered back.

"Do I have an aunt or uncle, too?" Hope blossomed in her expression.

Wanda shook her head. "No. Her dad passed away when she was still a kid, and her mom… Well, no one knows where she is. She took off the day after Brinn turned eighteen."

"Let me guess, Brinn's mother is dad's sister." She'd shut down again, losing all of the lightness she'd found during her Prince sing-along.

"Unfortunately, yes." The Danvers weren't ever going to win any awards for family values.

"Figures." A muscle in Blake's neck pulsed, making it clear she was doing her best to swallow her anger.

Wanda made a mental note to take her somewhere to work out her aggravation. Like an ax throwing bar or a boxing class at the gym.

As soon as they reached the two-person table, Wanda heard a feminine voice call, "Isn't that Wanda? Is she having lunch with us, too?"

Wanda turned to the left, her gaze landing on a pretty older woman with blond hair and a wide smile. Immediately her stomach dropped straight to her toes as she recognized the woman from Cameron's room at the inn.

"Wanda?" Cameron's voice filtered through the din of the other diners. A chair scraped on the floor, and when Wanda's eyes finally found him, he was already striding toward her, his hand out.

"Hey, Cam," she said, leaning into him as he wrapped one arm around her and kissed her cheek. "I didn't know you would be here."

"I spent the morning working with Miranda and now we're here having lunch with my parents." He waved at the group of people at a nearby table. "You and your sister should join us."

"I really don't—"

"It's no problem," Sadie said, already moving the chairs and pushing the smaller table up against the other one. She had the table set up in no time and then added, "I'll get you both some water and then take your drink orders."

Sadie was gone before Wanda could protest further. She glanced at the three other faces, each of them watching her expectantly. There was no way to bow out of the situation gracefully, so she took a seat across from her sister and said, "Hello, everyone. This is my sister Blake."

Once they'd all introduced themselves, Miranda moved over so that Cameron could sit next to Wanda. And that's when the torture started.

"Wanda, it's so nice to see you again," Emily Copeland said. "I'm just so embarrassed that we ruined your plans last night. I do hope you'll forgive us."

"What plans?" Miranda asked as she shoved a sweet potato fry into her mouth.

"Yeah, what plans?" Blake asked. "You should've told me if you had something to do."

More like *someone,* Wanda thought. She opened her mouth to brush them off, but Emily beat her to the punch.

"She was at the inn to surprise Cameron with a romantic evening, but I'm afraid we put a major dent in her plan." Emily chuckled softly. "Poor Cameron. I bet he never imagined that at his age he'd still be getting cockblocked by his mother."

"Mother!" Cameron sputtered, nearly spitting out the sip of beer he'd just taken.

Blake giggled. "Oh, oops. I also cockblocked him when he tried to surprised Wanda at her house."

The sound of Blake's laughter was music to Wanda's ears, and she decided in that moment that all of the embarrassment in the world was worth it as long as her sister was smiling.

"Can we stop talking about this now?" Cameron asked, wiping at his chin with a napkin.

"Now, Cam. It's nothing to be embarrassed about," his mom said, patting his arm. "I'd be more concerned if I knew you didn't have a sex life."

Blake let out a bark of laughter and then clasped her hand over her mouth as she turned bright red.

Wanda couldn't help it. She laughed, too.

"Can someone just put me out of my misery now?" Cameron asked. "A tranquilizer dart would do the trick."

"Please," Emily said, rolling her eyes at her son. "You're too old to be crawling under the table. We're all adults here… well, mostly." She winked at Blake. "There's nothing to be ashamed of."

"I'm not ashamed. I just don't want to talk about this with my mother," Cameron grumbled. "Miranda, help me out here. Tell them this isn't appropriate lunch conversation."

"Me?" Miranda placed a hand to her chest. "I'm a romance novelist, Cam. This right here? It's content gold. No way. I want to hear more about what happened when Emily interrupted the surprise."

"Nope!" Wanda said, sending Miranda a glare. "We're definitely not talking about that. Let's just say that I intended to surprise Cam. Instead, I was the one who got the surprise. Then, he tried to return the favor and ended up half naked in front of my sister. I think it's fair to say that last night wasn't in the cards for us."

"Oh, honey," Miranda said, laughing. "That is some seriously bad luck."

"You can say that again," Blake chimed in. "You haven't lived until you walk in on someone's booty call."

Emily let out a cackle and then raised her hand for a high five with Blake. "You got that right, sister."

Cameron's dad bent his head and chuckled softly.

Wanda turned to Cameron. "I'm starting to think maybe we should take off and just leave them to it."

"That sounds like a good idea. Make sure to take it *all off*," Miranda teased.

The rest of the table howled with laughter.

Wanda's entire body went up in flames with embarrassment. But still, she laughed along with them. She was more than happy to be the butt of the joke as long as it kept that twinkle in her sister's eye.

CHAPTER 6

Cameron picked up Miranda's latest bestselling release and pretended to read the back while he watched Wanda and Blake talk to Brinn. The bookstore clerk ran out from behind the cashier counter and wrapped her arms around a stunned Blake. When she pulled back, Brinn held Blake's arms and chattered excitedly while Wanda stood nearby watching over her sister.

After lunch, Cameron's parents had headed over to the Pelshes' winery for a tour and tasting of their limited-run wines. And when Wanda mentioned she and Blake needed to make a stop at Hollow Books, Cameron and Miranda hadn't hesitated to tag along. Miranda said she had books to sign, and Cameron had mumbled something about needing some new reading material.

Wanda had given him a skeptical look but hadn't called him out on his bullshit. Instead, she'd hung back, walking beside him while her sister chattered with Miranda about the first book she'd written, *Witching for You*. It had taken years, but it was finally being turned into a movie, and

Cameron, with Miranda's input, had been the one to write the screenplay.

"She's lovely, Cam," Miranda said, plucking her book from his hands. She opened it and scribbled her name on the title page before placing it back on the rack.

"Yes, she is," he said, still watching Wanda. Her red hair had a golden glow from the sun streaming through the front window, and Cameron thought she'd never looked so lovely.

"What are you going to do about it?"

He turned to look at his writing partner and frowned. "What do you mean, what am I going to do about it?"

She pushed a dark curl out of her eyes and smirked at him. "I mean, are you going to lock that down, or are you going to let this one slip away, too? Your track record for long-term relationships is rather poor, you know."

"How would you know?" He had only known Miranda for a few months. They were friends, but it wasn't as if he'd confided all of his deepest secrets.

"I know how to google, Cam. Famous people don't get to fly under the radar, even if they are only screenwriters." She squeezed his arm lightly. "I know all about the models and up-and-coming actresses you dated over the years. Wasn't your longest relationship like three months?"

"Seriously? What did you do, stalk me?" He took a step away from her, wondering if he'd made a grave miscalculation when he befriended her. "You're not going to break into my bedroom and leave a dead rabbit in my bed, are you?"

Miranda threw her head back and laughed. "No, darling. If I were to break into your quarters, I'd be more likely to leave a satchel of herbs that would curse your boy parts."

Cameron visibly cringed. "Tell me you're kidding."

Still chuckling, she bumped her shoulder to his and said, "Of course I am. I googled you when we started working together just to do my due diligence. Obviously, I didn't want to work with a loon." She winked at him. "There was one article that went off script from your career and detailed your love interests. I have to say that Wanda is a hundred times better than any of them."

"I agree," he said. The women he'd dated in Los Angeles had mostly been setups by friends. He'd given them all a try, but none had held his interest for longer than a few months. Which was perfectly fine with him. He hadn't been interested in anything long-term. The last time he'd let himself get invested in a woman, it had nearly broken him. It had taken months to put himself back together, and afterward he'd decided he wasn't going down that road again. But now, there was Wanda. And for some reason, he kept envisioning her ensconced in his bungalow in the Hollywood Hills. Permanently.

"Do yourself a favor and don't mess it up, Cam," Miranda said. "Make sure you don't let this one get away. You won't find another one like her."

No. He wouldn't. Wanda was fun, independent, and radiated joy. She wasn't interested in celebrity or status or his fancy house in the Hills. Wanda loved Keating Hollow, her friends, and her job. And she had a heart of gold. His world was just better when she was around.

"Are you listening to me?" Miranda prodded.

"I heard you." He glanced down at her, more than ready to end the conversation. "Don't you have to go harass Gideon now or something?"

"As a matter of fact…" She checked the time on her delicate wristwatch and then glanced at the door just as her boyfriend strode in, glanced around, and then headed straight for them. The Hollywood sheen he'd possessed had all but disappeared in the weeks since the man had moved to Keating Hollow. Instead of trousers and a button-down shirt, the man was now wearing worn jeans and a thermal Henley. His hands were stained with paint, and his hair had a casual, messy style that indicated he was a few weeks overdue for a haircut.

"Cameron. How's it going?" Gideon shook Cameron's hand. "Good to see you again. Did you and Miranda get the script worked out?"

"Yes, we did," Miranda answered for Cameron. She slipped her arm through Gideon's and started to pull him toward the door. "Now let's get out of here so Cameron can make his move."

"What move?" Gideon eyed Cameron again.

"Never mind." Cam shook his head at Miranda. "Get out of here. I'll call you tomorrow after I talk to the director."

"Bye!" Miranda wiggled her fingers at him and pulled her man out of the bookstore.

Cameron didn't even bother to pretend he was looking for books to read. Instead, he stood there, watching Wanda and admiring her backside in her jeans as he dreamed of getting her alone again.

It didn't take long for her to glance over at him. Their gazes locked, and it seemed to him as if everything and everyone else disappeared. There was only Wanda, and he desperately wanted her.

As if in a trance, Wanda walked toward him, her gaze never leaving his.

She stopped just in front of him and whispered, "You might want to stop looking at me like that."

He reached up and brushed a lock of hair out of her eyes. "Why's that?"

"Because if you don't, I might just rip your clothes off right here, and then we'll really be the talk of the town."

Cameron swallowed a growl. Then he pulled her into one of the aisles where they had a modicum of privacy and pressed her against one of the bookcases.

Wanda's breath caught as she lowered her gaze to his lips. "If you don't kiss me right now—"

He didn't give her a chance to finish her thought. Palming her cheeks, he covered her lips with his own and kissed her hungrily. She tasted of pears, and a hint of cherry, and pure desire.

Wanda melted into him, fisting her hand in his shirt.

Cameron's entire body came alive with unadulterated need. They'd had chemistry before, but now they were electrified. "Damn, Wanda. I'm half a second away from throwing you over my shoulder and hauling you back to my room at the inn."

She groaned and tightened her hold on him. "Our timing sucks."

He pulled back to look into her hazel eyes and caressed her cheekbone with his thumb. "Maybe we can work on that. Do you think you could get away for a few hours tomorrow for dinner?"

Wanda glanced over her shoulder toward the front of the store. When she turned back to him, she said, "Lunch would be better. I don't want to leave my sister on her own for dinner. She's had a rough time lately."

"Lunch it is." He pressed another kiss to her lips, this one gentle and lingering. "One?"

"At Woodlines?"

He grinned at her. "I was thinking more along the lines of a bedroom picnic. How about we meet at the new deli next to Mystyk Pizza, grab some sandwiches, and head back to the inn?"

"A bedroom picnic sounds perfect." She pressed up onto her toes, gave him one more searing kiss, and then hurried back to the front of the store with her face flushed and a grin on her lips.

CAMERON SAT at the small desk in his room at the inn, typing out a follow up email to the director of *Fire Valley,* the new series he and Miranda were working on. He'd sent the revised script over that morning, and within an hour the project had gotten the final green light they needed before they started casting. It was all great news, but the executive producer wanted him back in Vancouver early so they could get his input on casting. That meant he needed to leave the next morning, three days earlier than he'd expected.

That just meant he was going to need to make the afternoon count. After showering and tidying the room, he was just about to head out the door when his phone rang. Wanda's name flashed on the screen.

"Hello, gorgeous. Are you waiting? I was just on my way," he said into the phone as he reached for the doorknob.

"Uh, no," Wanda said. "I'm sorry, Cameron, but I'm not going to be able to make it today. There's been a situation here with Blake that I need to deal with."

All the joyful anticipation drained out of him as worry set in. "Is everything all right?"

"Yeah." She sighed. "I really am sorry. Blake's

grandmother is sick, and she's not dealing with it well. I think we're just going to stay in, watch movies, and bake cookies. An old-fashioned girls' day."

"I'm sorry she's having a rough time, but it sounds like you're handling it as well as you can." Was it crazy that Cameron was slightly jealous that he wasn't going to be the one helping her bake cookies? The very idea of spending a day with her in her home, chilling in front of a movie, was almost more enticing than the bedroom picnic he'd planned. Almost.

"I'm trying." He could hear the strain in her voice.

"Is there anything I can do?"

"Can we get a rain check?" she asked. "Maybe tomorrow? A brunch picnic would be great."

He couldn't hold back his groan of frustration. "I'd love to, but I need to be on a plane to Vancouver first thing in the morning. I just got the call an hour ago."

"Oh. Well, that's a bummer." She cleared her throat. "Do you know when you might be back in town?"

"A couple of weeks."

There was silence between them.

Finally, Wanda said, "Dinner when you get back?"

"Definitely." Disappointment clung to him as he cursed his producer. He'd waited weeks to see Wanda again, and he'd only gotten one lunch and a couple of stolen kisses.

"Call me tonight?" she asked. "I want to hear your voice again before you go."

"You got it."

After the call ended, Cameron shoved his phone into his pocket, and left his room. He had to move. Staying at the inn wasn't an option. If he did that, he'd spend the rest of the day brooding about his missed connection with Wanda.

He only got about a block down the street when his phone buzzed again. His heart swelled with the hope that it was Wanda and that she'd changed her mind or found time to see him before he had to leave. But when he looked at the screen, it was a number he didn't recognize. He frowned. Normally he didn't answer unknown calls, but with the movie still in production and the television show moving forward, he didn't have that luxury. The call was likely about one of the projects.

"Cameron Copeland," he said into the phone.

"Ah, Mr. Copeland?" a tentative voice asked.

He bit back a sigh. The person on the other end of the line sounded like an intern who hadn't yet figured out his job. "Yes. Who's this?"

"Cam Berry."

"Do I know you?" he asked, confused. But that last name certainly rang a bell. His college girlfriend's name was Tori Berry. Had she really named her son after him? And after the way she'd just dumped him? It didn't make any sense.

"No. We haven't met yet."

"Listen, Cam, I don't know what it is you're calling for, but I really don't—"

Cam's words came out in a rush as he cut him off, "I'm your son."

Cameron's entire body went ice cold, and he stood there on the sidewalk in the late winter sunshine in total shock. He must've heard incorrectly. "What?"

The young man on the other end of the line sucked in a breath. "My mom passed away six months ago, and when we were cleaning out her papers, I learned that you're my father."

A wave of panic rolled through Cameron. This wasn't

happening. How could it be? Surely Tori would've told him if he was a father, wouldn't she? A nagging voice in the back of his head reminded him that she'd walked out, leaving only a note that said, *Sorry*. Was this person on the other end of the line the reason she'd disappeared? "I don't understand. There must be some mistake."

"Listen, Mr. Copeland. I don't want anything from you. I just want to meet you."

Cameron's internal alarms were going off, but he forced himself to ignore them. If there was even a chance that this was true, Cameron needed to know the truth. "What did you find to make you think I'm your father?"

There was a pause, and then he said, "My original birth certificate."

CHAPTER 7

Wanda stood behind Blake, who was seated at the table in front of the computer watching as her Aunt Linda moved the computer screen so that Blake could Facetime with her grandmother. Despite the fun lunch and the time they'd spent with Brinn the day before, Blake had been having a rough morning. She'd woken from a nightmare but hadn't been willing to tell Wanda any of the details. Instead, she just kept insisting that she needed to speak to her grandmother. It had taken some convincing on Wanda's part, but Linda finally agreed to let them Facetime as long as Blake promised to not bring up the topic of moving back in with her.

Blake had started to argue, but Linda shut her down quickly. It was either promise to not talk about it or not talk to her at all. Finally Blake agreed, but she'd spent about thirty minutes ranting about it to Wanda.

"Hi, Grandma." Blake smiled into the camera and waved enthusiastically. "You look gorgeous today. Did you just get your hair done?"

The older woman smiled through the computer and pressed her hand to her freshly dyed auburn locks. "No. It's been a few months since I've seen Hal. He's such a genius. Always making me look my best."

Blake frowned. "Hal's moved to Vermont?"

Behind her mother, Linda shook her head and mouthed *no*. Then she leaned in toward her mother and said, "Actually, Mom, Vicki did your hair a few days ago. Remember? We went together and then had our nails done too."

"We did?" Grandma looked down at her fingers and surprise lit her clear blue eyes as she took in the bright red nails. "I guess we did." Lifting her hands, she showed off her manicure to Blake. "Linda's been so good to me. I'm going to be the bell of the ball at the church crab boil this weekend."

Blake chuckled. "You're always the bell of the ball, Grandma. It's nice your new church does crab boils, too. I know how much you love them."

"New church? No, dear. I'm still going to the same one I've always gone to. I'll be there as long as Pastor Kincaid is leading services. You know how much I like him. Your grandfather doesn't care for all the singing, but he deals with it."

Wanda's stomach clenched with dread. It was clear Blake's grandmother was having trouble remembering that she'd moved to Vermont to live with Linda. It wasn't even clear if she fully remembered that her husband had recently passed away. Linda definitely hadn't been exaggerating about the state of things with her mother. If anything, she'd undersold the situation.

"Right," Blake said, her voice shaky. "Pastor Kincaid does know how to hold an audience."

Wanda put a hand on her sister's shoulder and squeezed

gently for support. After a minute, Blake placed her hand over Wanda's and squeezed back.

The conversation went on for another ten minutes until Grandma got up and declared she had to get ready for a luncheon with her girlfriends. The ones she'd left behind when she moved.

When her mother disappeared from the room, Linda's pinched face filled the screen. "As you can see, she's not at all able to deal with a teenager. I'm sorry Blake, but you moving here or visiting right now just isn't an option. She has good days and bad days. Today is one of the bad ones. When she finds out there's no lunch with Patsy and Minnie, it's going to get even worse."

"I understand," Blake said, wiping at the tears pooling in her eyes. "Wanda said I can stay here."

"That's right," Wanda chimed in. "But I am going to need something that states I'm now her legal guardian so we can get her enrolled in school. Can you help us with that since your mom still has legal custody?"

Linda gave them a curt nod. "I'll call the lawyer and get it taken care of."

Then without warning, she ended the call, leaving them with a blank screen.

Blake glanced back at Wanda. "Well, that was rude. She didn't even say goodbye."

Wanda had to agree, but instead of perpetuating more animosity, she went for the tactful approach. "Yes, but I'm sure she's just stressed. At least you got to speak to your grandma."

Blake slumped in the chair and covered her face with her hands. "She's much worse than I thought. She thinks she's still in Maine and doesn't know that Grandpa died."

Wanda wanted to wrap the teenager up in her arms and physically hold her together, but she knew what Blake needed most was time to just work through her emotions. "I know, sweetie. I'm so sorry."

Her shoulders started to shake and then she let out a sob.

There was nothing Wanda could do but place her hands on her sister's shoulders and hold on. Make sure she knew she didn't have to go through any of this alone. Not as long as Wanda was around.

When Blake finally calmed, she turned and looked up at Wanda through red puffy eyes. "What am I going to do now?"

"Long-term, you're going to turn my second bedroom into your own teenage haven and enroll in school here in Keating Hollow. That's it. As long as you're in school, you don't have to do anything else except clean up after yourself. If you want to participate in extracurricular activities, go for it. If you want a part time job, that's cool too. Whatever works for you. Just no drinking, no parties, and no lying. If you follow those rules, we'll get along just fine."

Blake nodded and turned around, still slumped forward, looking completely dejected.

"As for what you're going to do today, how about we curl up on the couch and have a movie marathon? We'll watch some classic rom-coms like *Pretty Woman* or *Say Anything* or *Clueless*."

"Ugh, why those?" Blake asked. "I'd rather watch *Highschool Musical*."

Wanda laughed. "Okay. *Highschool Musical* it is. But first, we bake cookies. Double chocolate chip. And maybe brownies with a caramel layer."

"Baking and movies." Blake nodded slowly. A moment

later she gave Wanda a tired smile. "That sounds so... normal. I think the last time I baked anything was at Grandma's."

That had been over two years ago. Wanda's already aching heart felt like it cracked right down the middle. She couldn't even imagine what her sister's life had really been like while living with her parents. And now Wanda felt an overwhelming need to give her sister everything she'd never gotten from the two people who were supposed to love her the most.

Once Blake was set up in the kitchen and getting started on the cookies, Wanda slipped away and called Cameron to let him know she was going to miss lunch. Unfortunately, she also learned that he was leaving town again and their reunion would have to wait. She'd been disappointed but didn't regret her choices. Her sister needed her. End of discussion.

With a tray full of brownies and cookies, Wanda found *High School Musical* on one of her streaming channels and settled in on the couch with Blake. When it was done, they moved on to *Clueless* and *Mean Girls,* and then when they were in the middle of *Say Anything,* Blake curled in on herself and started to softly cry into a pillow.

"Hey," Wanda said, moving to sit next to her. "What's this about?" Of course she knew it had to be either about her parents ditching her or her grandmother's illness, but which one was anyone's guess.

"Everyone always leaves," she said through a quiet sob and burrowed further into her blanket.

Oh hell. Wanda glanced at the television, noting that the main character's father was just arrested, leaving his daughter on her own. Wanda should've known better. She should have paid more attention to the content of the movie. "Not everyone, Blake. I know it seems like that now, but you'll see. I won't leave. I'm permanent. Do you understand? I'll always be right here in Keating Hollow. You'll have me as long as you want me."

She quickly sat up, her eyes full of fire. "You forget I can read people, Wanda. Don't try to fool me."

Wanda jerked back, shocked. It was in her nature to defend herself, but she didn't want to push Blake away. She wanted to understand what it was she was thinking and feeling and reassure her if at all possible. "I haven't forgotten that you can read auras. But I do have to admit that I'm confused as to what you're sensing from me. Because from the moment you showed up on my doorstep, I've wanted to do nothing but keep you safe. I definitely don't want you to leave."

"Yeah." She squeezed her eyes shut and shook her head as if to clear her thoughts. "I get that. It's coming through loud and clear. There's big-sister protective energy vibes going on." She huffed out a humorless laugh. "You know who else gives off that energy when he isn't halfway through a bottle of Jack?"

"Our father?" Wanda guessed. He was the protective sort, but only when it suited him or when he wanted to impress someone. The moment someone became inconvenient, he pushed them aside and did whatever the hell he wanted.

She nodded and brushed her dark hair back. Narrowing her eyes at Wanda, she asked, "How can I trust that you won't do the same thing? That you won't push me aside for Cameron?"

"Cameron?" Wow. That was the last place she'd expected her sister to go. She and Cameron were just casual. They didn't even live in the same town. But since Wanda was Blake's only living relative that seemed to care about her, she supposed that Cameron would be threatening. Especially given her parents' history.

"What happens to me if you decide to run off and marry him? You'll move to Los Angeles, and I'll be where? Alone. Again. Then what?" There was defiance in her tone, but Wanda saw through it. Her sister was scared. Terrified. And why wouldn't she be? Wanda was her last living relative she could count on.

"Blake." Wanda sat up and turned to give her sister her full attention. "I will never leave Keating Hollow. It's my home. It's the place where I feel safe. My chosen family is here. My business is here. My home is here. And now *you're* here. Cameron… He's a really cool guy, but we aren't serious at all. He's not even my boyfriend."

"He wants to be," she said.

"He's also leaving to go to Vancouver tomorrow. I'm not even sure when I'll see him again. That's not a good recipe for a successful long-term relationship. Not that I'm even looking for that. But that's not what's important here. You need to know that I'm not our father. I'm not going to abandon you. Ever. You're my sister. I know we didn't grow up together, but you're important to me. And if you'll let me, I'd really like to earn your trust and prove that to you."

Blake didn't say anything. She just plucked at the blanket and eventually nodded.

Wanda squeezed her sister's hand and then let it go as she stood. "How about something other than sugar? Take out? I could call Mystyk Pizza and get delivery."

"Okay."

"Good. I'm dying for some cheesy goodness. Veggie? Meat Lovers? Chicken Alfredo?"

"Veggie." She smirked. "We have to eat something to combat those brownies."

Wanda chuckled and went in search of her phone to call in dinner.

WANDA PROPPED herself up on her pillows in her bedroom and listened to the babbling brook in the redwood painting. It was the last of Cameron's magic leftover from the night he'd tried to surprise her. She desperately wanted to run over to the inn just to see him one more time before he left. She knew without a doubt that if she didn't have Blake to worry about, she'd already be on her way. It wasn't just the physical relationship they shared that drew her to him. Wanda genuinely liked him.

But the fact that he lived in another city, had told her early on that he wasn't great at relationships, and had an unpredictable schedule meant that there really wasn't much sense in pursuing something with him. She recognized that he'd been willing to put the boyfriend label on whatever it was they were doing, but she couldn't do that now. Not with Blake in the picture.

Cameron was destined to walk out of her life. That, Wanda could handle. She was a big girl who knew what she wanted out of life. A man had never really been part of the equation. She was comfortable with that. Wanda had her friends and her career and a great town that never let her down. Her father had walked out on her, and ever since then, she'd been determined to not need a man in her life. She'd made room for one, but on her terms. Both she and Cameron had been perfectly fine with the way things had been going.

Now she had Blake to worry about. Not only was she worried about Blake getting close to him and then him leaving, as he was destined to do, she also just needed to focus on helping her sister feel safe. Now wasn't the time to start a long-distance relationship with anyone, much less a man who seemed to have as many commitment issues as she did.

Wanda slid down and buried her head under the covers so she couldn't see the babbling brook in the painting. Staring at it wasn't doing her any favors. Just as she started to drift off to sleep, her phone buzzed. Wanda groaned as she reached for it, already knowing who had sent the message.

CHAPTER 8

Cameron was still numb as he let himself into his room at the inn. Despite spending the day walking aimlessly around town, he still hadn't processed the phone call from Cam Berry. To say that he'd been blindsided would be an extreme understatement. How could it be possible that he had a son? How was it possible that Tori had been pregnant and never told him? Had she found out before or after she left?

His head was still spinning.

He had a son. A nineteen-year-old son.

Cameron was torn between hopping on a plane to San Diego to go meet him and running as fast as he could to Vancouver. He'd spent all afternoon trying to get his head around his new reality. Trying to make sense of Tori's decisions as he went over and over their breakup in his mind in an attempt to discover why she'd kept this from him.

Cameron had loved her. He'd wanted to marry her. When she left, she'd broken his heart. But why had she kept his child from him?

Rage rolled through him, and he wanted to scream. But at who? Tori was gone. None of this was Cam's fault. With no other outlet, Cameron changed into shorts, a T-shirt, and running shoes. In the next moment, he tore out of the inn and ran.

An hour later, dripping with sweat and physically exhausted, Cameron let himself back into his room. He'd worked out the anger, but the numbness was back. In a daze, he walked into the shower, hoping that when he reemerged, he'd have some clarity.

It didn't work.

He needed to talk to someone. He knew that. His parents were out of the question. Not yet. They'd ask him all the questions he couldn't answer. Then they'd want to meet Cam. There wasn't a doubt in his mind that they'd be thrilled to find out they were grandparents. Yes, they'd be upset they'd missed the first nineteen years of his life, but they'd waste no time making him a part of the family.

Was there something wrong with him that his first instinct wasn't to head straight to Southern California?

There was only one person he wanted to talk to.

Cameron picked up his phone and tapped out a text to Wanda. *Hey, gorgeous. Have a minute?*

When she didn't answer right away, he laid down on the bed and closed his eyes. But sleep was clearly out of the question. His mind wouldn't settle. Instead, he stared at the ceiling and tried to remember what was so important that he couldn't blow off Vancouver.

He didn't know how much time had passed when he finally heard his phone ping. But when it did, for some reason, he dreaded looking at the message. Still, he reached for the phone and tapped the notification.

Wanda: *I'm sorry, Cameron. I don't think it's a good idea for us to keep doing this. My sister needs me now, and it's better for both of us if we just let this go. We both know this was only temporary anyway. You're a great guy and a good friend. Good luck with your movie and the show. I'm sure they will both be wonderful.*

Cameron read the message three times before he turned his phone off, buried his face in the pillow, and let out an anguished scream.

IT TOOK three days for Cameron to call his son back. Three days to wrap his head around his new reality where he had a son and he wasn't seeing Wanda. He was still confused about the former, but he'd come to accept it. But the latter? He was still reeling. What had he done that had caused her to back off so abruptly? He understood her sister was going through a lot, but did that really mean they couldn't see each other? Obviously, the answer was yes, because Wanda hadn't minced words or left an opening for him to change her mind.

Once again, Cameron was in his hotel room, pacing. It was the first night he'd had off since he'd landed in Vancouver earlier in the week. In addition to being one of the main writers of *Fire Valley,* Cameron had also signed on as one of the producers, and he'd been tied up with casting and auditions. But now that he had a spare moment, he couldn't put off the inevitable any longer.

"Cameron?" His son said after picking up his call.

"Yeah. Sorry it's taken me so long to call you back. I—"

What could he say? I'm an idiot? That was probably the closest thing to the truth.

"Don't worry about it," Cam said. "I know my news was a shock."

"You can say that again." Cameron never thought he'd find himself in this position. He was a careful man. A responsible man. Though he hadn't had a long-term relationship since Tori, he'd always been honest about his intentions with anyone he got involved with. Which was why it was so baffling to him that he was still so raw over Wanda ending things with him. Especially when she was right. They'd both known it wasn't going to last.

"Um, is there a reason why you called?" Cam asked him.

Cameron nearly laughed. It sounded exactly like something he'd say to the jackass on the other end of the line who clearly didn't have a clue what he was doing. "Sorry. Yes. I guess I have questions."

"You guess?"

Leave it to his son to call him out on his bullshit. "Yes. I wanted to ask you about your mother."

There was a hesitation before he said, "All right."

"You said she passed away recently. Do you mind me asking what happened?"

"Cancer," he said, his tone void of emotion. "Stage four ovarian. She went quickly."

"I'm sorry," Cameron said as he closed his eyes and pictured the willowy blonde with the sweetest smile he'd ever seen. She'd been enchanting with her big wide eyes and slight frame. He'd wanted to keep her tucked to his side at all times, just to be near her. To hear her laugh, see her smile. He hadn't wanted to miss a minute.

"Yeah. Me, too."

Cameron blocked out the memories of his Tori and continued. "You said you just found out that I'm your father. Who did you think was your father?"

"Some football player that was killed in a car crash the night before he was supposed to be drafted. She gave me a picture of him, but that's all I know."

"Gavin Preston," Cameron said instantly. "He was her roommate's best friend."

"She didn't even tell me that much," Cam said, sounding annoyed. "I guess now I know why. If he wasn't really my father, why would she talk about him?"

Cameron's thoughts whirled. Tori had dated Gavin for a short time before they'd started their relationship. Had something happened between them before his tragic accident? Was that why she'd left? Had she secretly wished that Gavin was Cam's father? If so, why did she put Cameron's name on the birth certificate and name him Cam? None of it made sense, and he guessed that it never would. He needed to move on from trying to understand. The only thing that mattered was that he had a son. And waiting to meet him wasn't an option. "I'm not sure, Cam. I have a lot of questions for your mother, too, but since we're never going to get them answered, maybe we should just move forward."

"Sure, forward," he said. "How do we do that?"

"I'd like to meet you as soon as possible if you're up for it. I don't know about you, but nineteen years is too long for a father and son to wait to say hello for the first time."

"You want to meet?" He sounded shocked but pleased.

"Yes, I do. I'm tied up here in Vancouver for the next few days, but I should be able to fly out to San Diego after that. How does that sound?"

"Um, great, but I'm not in San Diego anymore."

"You're not? Where are you then?"

He let out a small chuckle. "Well, currently I'm in my VW bus, camping in the Santa Cruz mountains."

"Oh. I see. When will you be back in town?"

"Never?" The answer sounded like a question. "Actually, my mom's estate was finally settled. There wasn't much, just a bit of a nest egg. But the truth is there's really nothing keeping me there. So I decided to travel around a bit and figure out where I want to settle. After your mom told me about Keating Hollow, I decided to head there. I'm working my way north."

"You spoke to my mom?" Cameron gasped out. Had he told her she was a grandmother? If that news came from anyone other than Cameron, Emily Copeland was going to lose her ever-loving mind.

"Yes, but just to try and get in touch with you. She doesn't know… about me." Relief washed over Cameron, and he must've let out an audible sigh of relief since Cam shot back, "But she *is* my grandmother, and I'd like to meet her sometime. She seems really nice."

"Sorry." Cameron grimaced. "Of course you'll meet her. And my dad, too. I just want to be the one to tell them. They'll be ecstatic, but it's going to take a minute for them to adjust to the fact that they didn't know about you for nineteen years. That's all."

"Oh. Yeah. That part sucks."

"Agreed." Cameron sat in the desk chair in his room, feeling lighter than he had in three days. Just from talking with the kid over the phone, he liked him. He bet his mother had too. "So, did Emily talk your ear off when you spoke to her?"

He chuckled. "Definitely, but I didn't mind. Like I said, she's really nice."

"She is. You're going to love her."

Cam cleared his throat. "So… when do I get to meet her and your dad?"

"You're going to Keating Hollow, right?" The idea sounded just about perfect to Cameron. His parents were still there, and so was a certain redhead he couldn't get out of his mind.

"That's the plan."

"Then I'll meet you there. I have two more days here, then I'll be on the next plane. I'll call you when I get there. Does that work?"

"Definitely."

Cameron could hear the smile in his son's voice, and the sound made his heart swell and ache at the same time. It made him feel… whole. "Talk to you soon, son."

"You too, Dad."

When Cameron ended the call, he had a smile on his face and felt lighter than he had in days. He glanced around his room and decided he felt too good to be cooped up. After grabbing his hotel key, he headed down to the bar and ordered one of their microbrews on tap.

He'd just taken his first sip when a stunning brunette sat down next to him and called the bartender over.

"What can I get you?" the clean-cut young man asked her.

"This sweetheart of a man is going to buy me a martini," she said, winking at Cameron.

"You got it." The bartender went to work while Cameron eyed the flirtatious woman.

"That was pretty bold," he said, amused. He was no

stranger to being hit on, but this woman had some serious game. He couldn't help but admire her.

"My mama always taught me I had to go after what I wanted. There's no sense in waiting around for it. Right?"

He couldn't disagree with her. In fact, her words hit home. He needed to go after what he wanted. If he never told Wanda how he felt, how could he expect her to give him a chance?

The bartender returned with the woman's martini. Cameron didn't hesitate to hand over his credit card.

"Thank you." She raised her glass to his, clinking them together.

"You're welcome." He took a drink of his beer, wondering what she'd do next.

She raised her glass to her lips and watched him over the rim of the glass as she sipped on the drink. Then she placed the delicate glass down and turned to him. "So, tell me, handsome. What brings you to Vancouver?"

"Work. You?"

"Same." She eyed him curiously. "You don't look like you're here for the pharmaceutical conference."

"Neither do you," he countered.

"You're right. I'm in sales. Women's intimates." Her lips turned up into a sexy smile as if she expected this information to seal the deal with Cameron.

He just chuckled. "Seems like you have an interesting job."

She raised one eyebrow. "It is. You know what's more interesting?"

He downed the rest of his beer and then asked, "What's that?"

She moved her hand to her chest and ran her fingers over

the top button of her blouse. "Take me back to your room, and you'll find out."

Cameron dropped a tip on the bar as he stood up. When his companion moved to do the same, he said, "Thanks for the offer, but I'm already taken."

Then he strode off, already calling the executive producer to let him know Cameron would be rearranging his schedule.

CHAPTER 9

"I can't believe how gorgeous you are right now," Wanda said to her best friend Abby, who was walking toward her table at Incantation Café. "You know that pregnancy glow they talk about?"

"I've heard of it," Abby said with a huge grin. She placed two paper coffee cups and a pastry bag on the table and then sat across from Wanda.

"Well, you're not glowing. You're blasting sunshine that is making my eyes water. It's a little much. Think you can dial it back a little?" she teased.

"Stop. You're grossly over-exaggerating. I'm barely even showing. Wait until I've gained another forty pounds and really need an ego boost to make me feel better about myself."

"Noted," Wanda said with a laugh. "But I find it hard to believe you'll be anything but radiant."

"And this is why I love you." Abby took a sip of her herbal tea and grimaced. "You know, I used to really like tea, but this baby isn't having it. I think she's already addicted to coffee."

"How is that possible? You've been drinking tea ever since you learned you were pregnant. And she? Did you learn the sex, or is this your intuition again?" Wanda asked her.

"I drank coffee for four weeks before I realized I had a baby on board. It's not my fault she loves the stuff. I mean, can you blame her? It's only a thousand times better than tea. And no. We didn't learn the sex from the healer. But Miranda is convinced I'm having a girl, so I'm going with it."

"Miranda is an earth witch," Wanda said. "She can't tell what you're having." She glanced across the café at her sister, who was talking to Hanna about a possible part-time job. "You should ask Blake. She's a spirit witch. She might be able to tell just by your energy."

Abby tilted her head and studied Blake. "Maybe, but I don't care either way. I just used she because Miranda said something unprompted. It feels like a sign or something."

"Whatever you say, Abs." Wanda took a long sip of her coffee, enjoying the dark roast. It was one that Cameron had suggested, and she'd fallen in love with the blend.

"Okay, Wanda. Spill," Abby said, slapping her hands down on the table and staring her in the eye. "Something's wrong that you're not telling me."

Wanda glanced again at her sister. "I'm just worried about her is all."

"Understandable," Abby said slowly. "She's had a rough go of it, but she'll heal from this. Especially since she has the most awesome sister on the planet."

"Well, there is that," Wanda agreed with a nod.

"You just need to give her time to adjust. It'll work out. You'll see." Wanda was about to argue that it might take a little more than just time, but Abby leaned forward and said, "But that's not all that's bothering you, is it? Something else is going on. Is it Cameron? Do I need to kick his ass? I'm ready, baby bump or no."

"No," Wanda said, shaking her head. "Down girl. He didn't do anything wrong."

"So why do you look like you want to cry into your cheese Danish?" Abby asked.

Wanda took a deep breath. "Because I broke things off with him through a text."

Abby leaned forward and hissed, "You did *what?*"

"You heard me. It's better to end it now before someone gets hurt." Wanda's gaze landed on her sister again. "I can't let anyone into her life who's just going to leave. She's had too much of that."

Abby sat back and studied her friend with her arms crossed over her tiny belly.

"What, Abs? I'm just trying to do what's right. Cameron and I… We were just messing around. It was fun, and yes, I liked him. But it was going nowhere. That was fine when it was just me. Now things are different."

"Are you certain it was going nowhere?"

"Yes. No doubt about it." Wanda didn't second guess her choices often. She was a full steam ahead, make the best of every situation kind of person. This was no different.

"Uh-huh. We'll see." Abby glanced at the magical window display and seemed to lose herself in the animated cookies that were shaped like daisies and dancing around in anticipation of an early spring.

"I know what you're doing," Wanda said, slumping back into her chair. "You might as well just say whatever it is that's on your mind. We both know that if you don't, you're going to obsess about it and then call and wake me up at midnight so you can get it off your chest."

Abby turned back to her friend and chuckled. "I would do that, wouldn't I? You know me too well."

Wanda nodded and waited.

"Okay, you want to know what I'm thinking? Well, here it is." She leaned forward again and said, "I think you're making a huge mistake by letting him go."

"Abs—"

"Nope. You wanted to hear what I have to say. Well, here it is. I've never seen you happier than when you were with Cameron. You know this glow you keep talking about me having? When you're with Cameron and you forget anyone is watching, you have one, too. He makes you happy."

"I'm always happy," Wanda insisted, trying to ignore the dull ache in her chest. It hurt to have her friend confirm what she'd been trying to ignore.

"Of course you are. That's your personality. But what you have with Cameron is different. If you just let him walk away without trying, I really think you'll regret it."

Wanda sucked in a deep breath and shook her head slightly. "You don't understand, Abby. I let him go because of Blake. She needs stability. And I need to make sure she knows that she's the most important person in my life. You can see that, right? After everything she's been through?"

"Sure," Abby said, furrowing her brow. "I guess I don't understand why that means you can't ever see Cameron again. It's not like you're the type to lose yourself in a man. You've always been fiercely independent. Why would that change now?"

"It wouldn't, but this isn't about me. Or even Cameron. It's about my sister, who has watched every single person in her life walk right out of it. And her mom has always chosen our father over her. It really messes with a person. So, I figure the least I can do is be her safe space where she doesn't have to worry about any of that."

Abby let out a sigh and shook her head. "I'm not sure how healthy that is, but I do understand where you're coming from." She reached across the table and squeezed her friend's hand. "I admire you for caring so deeply about your sister. You know that, right?"

Wanda gave her friend a tiny smile. "It's nothing you haven't done for Olive, even before she was your stepdaughter. Or for Hope when you discovered she was your sister. It's just who we are, Abby. We protect our own."

THE WINTER SUN streamed through the window of Wanda's small office. After her coffee date with Abby, she'd left Blake in her friend's care and had gone into work to return some emails and phone calls and to catch up on some paperwork. Keating Hollow was a relatively small village, and she was the only real estate agent within twenty miles. That meant she always had work piling up. With her sister in town, she'd been slacking more than usual.

She'd gotten through three voice mails and was typing out an email to confirm a short-term rental when the phone rang.

"Wanda Danvers. How can I serve your real estate needs today?"

"Oh, good. You're there," a familiar female voice said, but Wanda had difficulty placing her.

"I'm here," she said brightly. "What can I do for you?"

The woman chuckled. "This is Emily Copeland. Cameron's mother?"

"Of course." Wanda sat back in her chair and tried to ignore the sudden tension in her shoulders. Was she calling about her son? Talk about awkward. Wanda decided to go full-on professional as if she hadn't been sleeping with the woman's son the past few weeks. "Nice to hear from you again, Emily. How is your stay in Keating Hollow going? Have you made it to our spa, A Touch of Magic yet? The Townsend girls really know how to pamper a person."

"As a matter of fact, I was just in there this morning. My back has never felt better, and as a bonus, my toes are sparkling in pink. It was fabulous. Thanks for the recommendation. I'm going in next week to get my eyelashes and brows dyed."

"Next week?" Wanda asked, surprised. "Did you decide to extend your visit here? I seem to recall you were planning to only stay a few more days."

"Yes, we have. That's actually why I'm calling." There was a rustle as if Emily had covered the phone receiver, followed by a muffled voice that sounded like she said something about telling Cam later. "Sorry," she said when she came back on the line. "Dayton was asking me a something. Now, where was I?"

"You were just getting to the part about why you were calling."

"Right." She chuckled. "It's funny how easily the mind goes on vacation when you're excited about something, isn't it?"

"Sure," Wanda agreed, wondering if the woman was ever going to get to the point.

"Dayton and I have decided to stay in Keating Hollow

through the fall. I was wondering if you could help us find an apartment or cottage to rent instead of staying at the inn. It's lovely here, but we could use a kitchen of our own and some outdoor space."

"You've decided to stay?" she asked, stunned. That was unexpected. And disconcerting. Did that mean Cameron would be spending more time in her town? Suddenly he had more ties to Keating Hollow than just Miranda.

"Yes. This town is just so enchanting. We're actually considering moving here, but we want to spend some extended time first to make sure it's the right move for us."

"That's… fantastic," Wanda said, already clicking on her file of short-term rentals. "I'd be glad to help you out. There aren't a lot of seasonal rentals available, but if you let me know what your parameters are, I can get a list together and start showing you the properties this afternoon or tomorrow. Whatever works for you."

"Perfect. It has to have at least two bedrooms. Three would be better, but as long as there's a guest room for Cameron it will work. Outdoor space. A patio, deck, or balcony, somewhere we can sip wine and enjoy the evenings this summer. And if it has a view of the river or the valley, even better."

Wanda finished scribbling her list on a notepad and tried to block out the mention of Cameron. It was official. He'd be back, sooner rather than later.

"I think that's it," Emily said. "Think we might find something?"

Wanda quickly scanned her list and grimaced. Most of the rentals were already booked, and the ones that were left were small and in need of some updates. "I'll do my best," she said anyway, hoping she could drum up some possibilities.

"Give me until tomorrow to do some research. Does ten o'clock work?"

"Absolutely. Should we meet at your office?"

"How about Incantation Café?" It would be Saturday and Blake's first day at work, and Wanda wanted to make an appearance to show her support.

"Perfect. See you then."

The line went dead. Wasting no time, Wanda got out her phone directory and started making calls.

Two hours later, feeling rather pleased with herself, Wanda closed her laptop and started to lock up for the day. Just as she was about to turn the lights off, the door opened and a young man who looked to be in his early twenties walked in.

"Hi," he said, running a hand through his thick dark hair. "Are you Wanda Danvers?"

"That's me," she said, smiling at him. He had piercing blue eyes, golden skin, and a face that should have been gracing magazine covers. He was so handsome he didn't even seem real, except for the fact that he was dressed in a faded Guns N' Roses T-shirt, ripped jeans, and sneakers that had seen better days. "And you are?"

"Cam Berry." He held out his hand. "I hear you're the one to ask if I'm looking for a place to rent."

Wanda nodded as she shook his hand. "Short-term or long-term?"

"Long-term, but a month-to-month lease would be ideal."

"Okay." Wanda slipped back behind her desk and gestured for him to sit down. "I'll do my best, but just to warn you, Keating Hollow is pretty low on rental inventory. What are you looking for?"

"Anything as long as it has a hot shower, a place for a bed, and a small kitchen," he said. Then he added, "I'm not picky as long as the rent's cheap."

Wanda pursed her lips and nodded. She'd been in his shoes once right after her mother died. She'd been on her own for the first time ever, and if it hadn't been for a sweet older neighbor letting her rent the apartment above her garage, Wanda didn't know where she would've ended up. "Got it. I'm sure we'll find something. You'll need at least the first month's rent and a security deposit. First and last would be better."

He bit down on his bottom lip. "It depends on how much, but I do have some money saved."

"Good deal." She pulled out an information worksheet and handed it over to him. "Fill this out and we'll see what we can find."

As she'd suspected since Cam was new in town, he didn't have a job. His first order of business was to find a place to stay.

"What kind of work are you looking for?" Wanda asked as she printed out a few possibilities.

"Construction. I've worked for my friend's dad for the past four summers. I would've stayed on with him, but he retired and shuttered the business. That gave me the opportunity to travel a little, and here I am."

"You couldn't have picked a better place if I do say so myself." She winked at him. "And it just so happens that you're in luck. Keating Hollow is currently experiencing a population growth and has several new builds going on."

"Really? Can you point me to any construction crews? I'd like to see if any of them are hiring."

"I can do better than that." She grabbed her phone, sent a text, and a moment later asked him, "Are you free now?"

“Sure.”

Wanda ushered him out the door and guided him toward her golf cart.

“This is sweet. Love the surround sound,” Cam said.

“It’s everyone’s favorite part. Buckle up. I just put a turbo booster on this thing.” Wanda pressed the accelerator to the floor of the cart, and the pair of them raced down Main Street.

By the time the sun started to set, Cam had a job working for Hunter McCormick’s construction crew and a place to live in the garage apartment on Gideon Alexander’s property that he was renovating. They’d worked out a deal where Cam could live in the apartment in exchange for labor on the remodel.

“Wow,” Cam said when Wanda dropped him off in front of her office. “Did that just really happen?”

She grinned at him. “They don’t call Keating Hollow an enchanted village for nothing. Just make sure you show up on time and do a good job. Got it?”

“No need to worry about that.” He hopped out of the golf cart and came around to Wanda’s side with his arms outstretched. “Can I give you a hug for being so awesome?”

“Of course.” Wanda wrapped her arms around the young man. His heartfelt thanks was just the jolt of cheer she needed. Life was hard sometimes, but this was a reminder that it was also beautiful. She never felt better than when she was able to do her part in helping someone who needed it.

“Thanks again, Wanda,” he said as he strode toward a vintage white VW camper van. “I won’t forget this.”

“You’d better not,” she called after him. “I expect cupcakes every Friday morning for a month.”

“I’m on it.”

CHAPTER 10

"You did what?" Cameron gasped out as he stared at his parents, wondering if they'd eaten a magic mushroom or an enchanted cookie from the herbal shop. "I thought you were traveling to Europe this summer. What happened to gondola rides in Venice and touring the Louvre?"

Cameron had arrived late in the afternoon on Monday and immediately invited his parents out to dinner at the Cozy Cave. He needed to tell them about Cam as soon as possible. But right after they'd been seated and before he'd been able to break the news, his mother excitedly told him about the house they'd rented for the remainder of the year.

"We were just going to stay through the fall, but then Wanda was telling us all about the recent Christmas ball, and we really just don't want to miss out on anything," Emily explained. "It's better if we get the full experience before we commit."

"Commit to what? And what about Europe?" he asked

again, trying to figure out exactly what had happened in the week that he'd been gone.

"To moving here of course," Emily said as if that had been the plan all along.

"Wait. You're moving to Keating Hollow? Permanently?" Cameron asked, his gaze shifting between his parents.

"We're thinking about it," Dayton said. "Your mother and I have been on the lookout for somewhere special to move for a while now. We're tired of the desert. Palm Springs is a wonderful community, but we'd rather be somewhere closer to nature."

"And Keating Hollow is the place?" He wasn't sure why he was so hesitant about their choice to test out the magical village. If anything, Palm Springs had never really been the right fit for them. It had a witch community, but not a close-knit one like Keating Hollow. The people in this town looked out for each other; down south, they mostly stuck to themselves. Even their closest friends had moved back East after they'd both retired.

"We think it might be. Don't you? Remember, you're the one who told us how special it was," Emily said, eyeing him with suspicion. "Or is there a reason you don't want us here?"

"That's not it," Cameron said, picking up his water glass and downing half of it. "I'm just surprised. That's all. Are you canceling your trip to Europe then?"

"Yes," Emily said. "Your father wasn't all that thrilled with taking another transatlantic excursion so soon after our trip to England and Ireland last fall. I agreed to change plans as long as we're able to stay here in the redwoods."

It was true that Cameron's father really only traveled to make his mother happy, and that staying in Keating Hollow and being close to the ocean was much more his speed. "Well then, I think that's great."

"We rented a place with a bedroom for you, Cameron," Emily said. "You're welcome to stay with us whenever you're in town visiting Wanda. I know it's not cool to stay with your parents, but the guest room is downstairs with its own separate entrance. We shouldn't cramp your style *too* much."

"Uh, Wanda and I aren't exactly seeing each other anymore," he muttered and then immediately regretted it. He should've just left it alone. His mother would've figured it out sooner or later.

"Why? What happened?" she asked, concern lacing her tone. But when he didn't answer, her expression turned stormy. "Cameron, what did you do? Please tell me you didn't do something to hurt that lovely girl."

"No, mother. Of course not," he said. "It's nothing like that. She's busy with her sister and I'm... temporary at best. She thinks it's better if we're just friends."

"Well, that's the dumbest thing I've ever heard," Emily said.

"Now, dear." Her husband placed his hands over her fingers. "I'm sure Wanda has her reasons."

Yeah. Cameron wasn't stable enough for her. The worst part was that he couldn't even disagree. His track record spoke volumes.

"She'll regret it," Emily said, shaking her head. "I saw the way she looks at you, Cam. That's not the look of someone who is just interested in being friends."

A dull ache formed just over Cameron's right eye. He needed to exit this conversation immediately. "Mom, I didn't come here to talk about Wanda. There's something else you need to know."

His mother blinked at him. "Are you all right?"

"Yes. I'm fine. In fact, this is good news. I think you're going to be very happy."

"Oh." A smile claimed her lips and she leaned forward. "You know how I love good news. Let's hear it."

"You know that phone call you got from Tori's son?" he asked, wiping his sweaty palms on his jeans.

"Yes. Did you finally call him back?"

He shook his head and for the first time wondered how Cam had gotten his number. If his mom had given it out, she'd have told him… right? On second thought… He stared her in the eye and said, "He called me."

"Oh, really? That's interesting." She gave him a self-satisfied smile, confirming his suspicions. Normally he'd be really irritated that she'd given out his private number, but in this case, he was only grateful. He couldn't regret finding out he had a son.

"Mom." Cameron shook his head.

"Oh, honey. He just seemed so sweet, and he didn't say one word about Hollywood. I got the impression it was something personal about his mother. Please, tell me I was right."

"You were right. In fact…" Cameron took a deep breath and said, "It turns out that Tori was pregnant when she left but didn't bother to tell me."

"Pregnant?" his father asked. "You got that girl pregnant? Cameron. How many times did we have the protection talk? I thought you knew better than that."

"Dayton," Emily scolded. "Cameron is nearly forty years old. He doesn't need a lecture about safe sex. Especially since it's too late now."

"Says the woman who told her son to glove up right before he left for a booty call last week," Dayton muttered.

"Excuse me," Cameron said, completely ignoring their comments. "Do you think we could get back on topic now?"

"We were on topic, dear. We were discussing your lack of safe sex." She smiled up at the waiter who'd just arrived with a round of drinks and their appetizers.

He was a young man who couldn't be any older than Cam, and when he looked at Cameron, he snickered. "I guess these talks never get easier, huh?"

"You can say that again."

He laughed and placed a bowl of chowder in front of each of them.

Once the waiter was gone, Emily dipped her spoon into her bowl and said, "Finish the story, Cameron. What happened? Did Tori have the baby?"

Cameron nodded. "She did. He didn't know I was his father until he found his original birth certificate. Cam Berry is my son, and he's already here in Keating Hollow."

Emily dropped her spoon and stared at Cameron with her mouth open. "Victoria had your child and never told you?"

He nodded, trying to ignore that dull ache in his gut. It appeared every time he thought about all the years he'd missed with Cam. "Wasn't that your first thought when I said she was pregnant when she left me?"

His mother shook her head. "Honestly, no. I thought maybe she lost it or… well never mind." Her face turned red as her lips twisted in anger. "I cannot fathom a woman having a child and not having the decency to tell the father. What the hell was she thinking? How could she do this to you?" She turned to look at her husband. "To us?"

Dayton moved his chair to sit closer to his wife and wrapped an arm around her. "Take a deep breath, Em. I know you're upset. So am I. But Victoria is gone now. We're not going to get answers to those questions." Dayton raised his head and met his son's gaze. "Right, Cameron? You don't know why she didn't tell you?"

Tears stung Cameron's eyes, but he blinked, willing them to disappear. He would not break down in front of his parents. He'd let go of Tori a long time ago. He was over it. Wasn't he? Then why did it hurt so much to talk about her? He took a breath and answered his father. "I honestly have no idea. Tori knew I wanted to marry her. Up until she left, I thought she wanted that, too. If she'd told me about the pregnancy, I would've proposed on the spot, and I sure as hell would've been there for her and Cam."

"That's what I thought," Dayton said with a confident nod. "You said Cam is here in Keating Hollow?"

"Yes. I'm going to meet him tomorrow after he gets off work."

"Oh." Emily pressed a hand to her heart. "I so wish I could be there."

"Uh, I don't think that's a good idea, Mom. It's going to be overwhelming enough for the two of us as it is. Do you think you could give me a few days before I introduce you?"

"Of course," she said quickly, waving a hand. "You're right. I just... How old is he?"

"Nineteen."

"I've missed nineteen years of my only grandson's life. I don't want to miss any more."

Cameron scooted over, and just like his father had done, he wrapped his arm around her. "You're in luck then, because he's just moved to Keating Hollow. So while you two are figuring out if it's your permanent home, you should have plenty of time to get to know him."

She sniffed. "I hope he likes lots of hugs and grandma attention, because he's about to get a lot of both."

Cameron laughed. "I hope so too."

CHAPTER 11

The day had been a complete loss. Cameron had spent some time trying to tweak a couple of the *Fire Valley* scripts that would come later in the season, but when he realized he couldn't concentrate, he switched to fielding business emails. After he replied to the wrong person, accidentally deleted an important communication, and then misspelled public, resulting in a line that read *convene in a pubic space*, he gave up completely.

Instead, he got into his running gear and took off into the redwoods, determined to pound away the growing anxiety.

By the time he walked into Incantation Café at just after five in the afternoon, he felt as if the day had lasted for fifty-two hours already. He took a moment to settle himself and then glanced around the lobby.

Cam said he'd be wearing a Metallica T-shirt and jeans. It didn't take long to spot him. He was sitting at a table, laughing with Blake. That was interesting. His nerves fled, and he walked over to the table.

"I hope I'm not interrupting," Cameron said as he stopped in front of them.

"Cameron. Hey. I didn't know you were back in town," Blake said, waving her hands animatedly and smiling up at him. "Does Wanda know you're back?"

He shook his head. "Not yet. I've been a little busy." His gaze darted to the young man sitting across from her. A lump formed in his throat as he laid eyes on his son for the very first time. He was a good-looking kid, and even on first glance, there was no mistaking that he was a Copeland. The kid was the spitting image of Dayton Copeland when he was that age.

Cameron held his hand out. "Hello, Cam. It's nice to meet you."

His son stared up at him, his eyes wide and frozen like a deer in the headlights.

"Cam?" Blake prompted. "You okay?"

"Yeah." He stood, and instead of shaking Cameron's hand, he pulled the man into a hug.

Cameron's arms went around his son, and in that moment his heart seemed to burst wide open. They stood there for a long moment, just holding onto each other. Cameron didn't want to let him go and eventually chuckled to himself.

Cam was the one to finally pull back and ask, "What's funny?"

"Your grandmother is going to be thrilled that you're a hugger."

His son chuckled. "Is that right? Should I be scared?"

"A little bit." Cameron grinned at him and then turned his attention to Blake. "I didn't know you knew my son. How long have you two been friends?"

"Son?" Blake echoed then looked at Cam. "Cameron is your father? Is that why you moved here?"

Cam nodded. "One of the reasons. I've been looking for a new place to settle for a few months now. Keating Hollow just seemed… right." He gazed at her and added, "Seems that was a good choice. I wouldn't have met you otherwise."

She blushed and then got up and said, "I'll let you guys catch up. She turned to Cameron. "Nice to see you again, Mr. Copeland."

"Please, call me Cameron. It was nice to see you again, too, Blake."

They both watched her slide back behind the counter where Hanna, the owner of the café, was waiting to finish Blake's training.

Cameron took Blake's seat. "That was quick."

"What was?" Cam asked him, looking confused.

"Blake. How long were you in town before you asked her out?" Cameron asked.

"I didn't ask her out. We're just… friends." He glanced over at her and let his gaze linger before finally looking back at Cameron.

Friends. Sure. Cameron was well aware of what that look meant. It was the same one he wore when he looked at Wanda. "Listen, Cam. Blake is new in town—"

"I know. She told me. It's part of the reason we've formed a friendship. Two outsiders. You know how it is."

"Sure." It made sense that they were drawn to each other. No one liked being the outsider. There was also the fact that they were both going through big losses in their young lives. "Just do me a favor and be careful, okay? She's gone through a lot and could really use someone to look out for her."

Cam frowned. "Blake looks like she can take care of herself."

"I agree, but everyone could use someone who has their back every now and then."

"Don't worry about that," Cam said. "I've got it covered."

"Glad to hear it." Cameron sat back in his chair and studied his son. The resemblance really was striking. "I can't wait for you to meet your grandfather. You look exactly like him."

"Oh yeah? Does he have unruly curly hair, too?"

Cameron chuckled. "He did once. Now he's mostly bald."

"Great. Something to look forward to." Cam's eyes sparkled with amusement, and Cameron did everything he could to memorize the moment.

The pair spent the next hour learning about each other's lives. Cameron was a little disappointed to learn that his son hadn't even had the opportunity to go to college, and instead, learned construction from a friend's father.

"You know, if you ever do want to go to school, I can help with that," Cameron said.

His son's smile vanished, and his eyes narrowed. "Why?"

Cameron straightened at the obvious hostility. "Why not?"

"Because I already have a trade. Is there something wrong with being in construction?"

Woah. Cameron had definitely stepped on a landmine. "No. Nothing at all. If that's your passion, then great. Lucky you that you've figured out what you want to do already. I only offered because you said you didn't have the option. I happen to have the resources to offer it as an option if you want. If you don't, no problem. I just want you to have the choice."

"That's... noble of you," Cam said, his voice flat.

"It's not noble. It's just the right thing to do. You're my son. It's my job to help you succeed in whatever it is you want to succeed in." Where was this coming from? All Cameron had said was that he'd pay for college if Cam wanted to go. What was so terrible about that?

"I didn't come here for your money, Cameron," his son said. "I came to meet the man listed on my birth certificate. I don't need you to ease your conscience for not being around by throwing money at me. That's not what I'm about." He sat back and folded his arms over his chest, looking defiant.

"That's not..." Cameron took a moment to think about what he wanted to say. How had this conversation gone south so fast? "This isn't me easing my conscience. The truth is I had no idea you existed. Your mother never told me. We hadn't even talked about having kids. I loved her, but we were still kids, ourselves, kids who were still in college. Then she broke it off and I never saw her again. Not even around school. Someone told me she transferred, and that was the end of our relationship. So guilt? No. That's one emotion I don't feel. Just about the only one. There's a storm of others going on inside of me though. Joy, wonder, fear, anger, and disappointment are just a few."

"Anger? Why are you mad?" Cam asked. "Did I piss you off already?"

"I'm not angry at *you,* Cam. I'm angry at your mother for keeping you from me. I keep going over our relationship in my mind and trying to pinpoint one reason why she wouldn't have told me, and I've got nothing. But one thing's for certain, if she had told me, I'd have never let her walk away from me like that. I would've been in your life no matter what happened between me and your mother."

"You would've?" Cam's hardened expression vanished and was replaced by one of sheer surprise.

"No question," Cameron said.

"Do you have any other kids?" his son asked.

Cameron raised one eyebrow. "Not that I know of."

Cam chuckled at that. "Here's hoping you don't have another one of me showing up on your doorstep."

"It wouldn't be the worst thing in the world."

"It wouldn't?"

"Nope," Cameron said. "It turns out that I like you and the idea of being a dad. I just wish the circumstances had been different. I would've liked to have been at your baseball games—"

"Soccer," Cam interrupted.

"Right. I would've liked to have been at your soccer games, taken a thousand cheesy pictures for your prom, tormented you about your first girlfriend—"

"What if she was a he?" Cam asked, clearly testing him.

"Or boyfriend. Whichever. I don't care who you date as long as they aren't a hoodlum."

"Tell me you didn't just say hoodlum," Cam said, laughing. "You're not *that* old, are you?"

"I'm old enough," Cameron said, pleased to see the tension between them had eased.

"Why are you looking at me like that?" Cam asked.

"Like what?"

"Like you're planning my future or something. It's making me a little uneasy to be honest."

"That's not what I was doing," Cameron said. "Actually, I was just thinking about how I'm not interested in putting any expectations on you. I just want to get to know you and do all the things a good parent should. Like provide for schooling if that's your path, or help you start a business, or just be there for moral support. Hell, I don't know. I've never done this. I just want to be the person who's there for you, the way my parents are for me. I know without a doubt that if I needed them, they'd be there no matter what. And that's what I want to be for my own son."

"That's… a lot to take in," Cam said.

"So is finding out you're a parent. But I'm dealing with it." His lips twitched into a small smile.

"Yeah, I bet. Well, I guess if you can adjust, then I can too. But you'll probably need to give me a minute since we just met. Don't expect me to spill all of my secrets just yet."

Cameron let out a bark of laughter. "Please. I'm taking a lot of my own secrets to my grave. There are just some things you never tell your parents, no matter what."

"Then we understand each other."

Cameron offered his hand again, and this time Cam shook it. They had an understanding now, and that was more than Cameron could've hoped for.

They kept talking until Hanna came over and said, "Sorry, boys. You don't have to go home, but you can't stay here. It's closing time."

Cameron glanced at his phone and was surprised to see they'd been sitting in the café for over three hours. "Damn, sorry, Hanna. I didn't even order anything." He reached for his wallet, intending to at least tip her for the use of her establishment, but she stopped him and shook her head.

"You'll make up for it next time," she said as she led the two men and her new employee to the door.

"Got it. Thanks, Hanna. See you tomorrow." He slipped out the door and was blasted with a stream of cold air. The weather had been mild earlier in the day, but the temperatures had dropped considerably. He turned to Cam. "Do you need a ride somewhere?"

"Nope. I've got my wheels." He gestured to the white VW bus parked right in front of the café.

"Right. Well, goodnight. I'll be in touch. Emily is going to want to meet sooner rather than later."

"I can't wait," Cam said and held his hand out to Blake. "Ready to go?"

"Definitely. I'm beat." She waved at Cameron and climbed into the old bus. A few seconds later, Cam fired up the engine and took off down Main Street.

As he watched the lights disappear into the distance, he pulled out his phone and called Wanda. Her phone went straight to voice mail. Disappointment settled around him. He hadn't been planning on calling her, but after spending the afternoon with his son, she was the only person he wanted to talk to about it.

"Hey, Wanda. It's me, your favorite Hollywood screenwriter. It turns out I'm back in Keating Hollow sooner than expected, and there's a lot I want to tell you. If you're free tonight, can you give me a call? I'd really like to talk to you about it."

He ended the call, shoved his hands into his pockets, and walked the short distance to the brew pub. After the day he'd had, a beer sounded just about perfect.

CHAPTER 12

Wanda sat on her couch staring at her phone. She'd been in the shower when Cameron called, and ever since she'd listened to the message, she'd been trying to decide if it was a good idea to call him back. He'd sounded good. Really good. And she desperately wanted to know why he was back in Keating Hollow so soon. But she'd meant it when she said they should end their affair. If she called him back, her resolve would crumble. There was no doubt about it.

When she heard Blake's key in the door, she turned off the rock documentary she'd been ignoring and waited to greet her sister.

Blake walked in with her hands full of takeout.

"Hey. How was work?" Wanda asked.

Her sister let out a tiny gasp and jumped, clearly startled by Wanda's presence. "Holy crow, Wanda. Why are you sitting in the dark like that? Were you trying to give me a minor heart attack?"

"I'm not sitting in the dark," Wanda insisted as she

glanced around. But when she realized Blake was right, she chuckled. “Oops. I had the television on, so I guess I didn’t notice when the light changed.”

“You’re a mess.” Blake moved toward the kitchen. “Are you hungry? I got calzones from Mystyk Pizza.”

“Yes.” Wanda jumped up and followed Blake. After grabbing some drinks, they sat down at the table and dug in. “This is delicious. Did you buy Cam dinner as a thank you for chauffeuring you around?”

“I tried, but he wouldn’t let me.” She took a small bite of her calzone and then added, “I guess it shouldn’t be a surprise considering Cam is short for Cameron, but I didn’t realize that Cameron is his dad. Now I feel a little weird because I saw his father half naked.”

Shocked, Wanda sucked down a piece of calzone and started coughing. Tears stung her eyes as she tried to get her breathing under control as she forced out, “What?”

“You didn’t know?” Blake asked, frowning.

Wanda shook her head and coughed some more.

“Jeez. Are you all right? Do you need the Heimlich or something?”

“No,” Wanda wheezed and finally sucked in a clear deep breath. “Sorry. Calzone misfire.”

“I guess so.”

“Are you sure Cameron is Cam’s father?” Wanda asked, completely confused. If that was true, then Cameron had lied to her. But why? Did he have an entire family he didn’t want her to know about? No. That couldn’t be right. She’d met Cameron’s parents. Surely if he was married or carrying on with someone else, they would’ve had a problem with finding an almost naked woman in his bed. Wouldn’t they?

“Yep. I was sitting with Cam on my break at the café

when Cameron came in and referred to Cam as his son. Then they spent the rest of my shift talking as if they hadn't seen each other in a long time."

Wanda concentrated on her food, trying to control the bubbling rage streaming through her veins. Why had he lied? It didn't make any sense to her. They'd talked about their histories. Wanda had even asked if he'd ever been married or had kids. His answer had been no. And when she asked if he'd ever gotten close to popping the question, he'd said yes and told her a little about his college relationship. She'd told him that was closer than she'd ever gotten.

"Wanda?" Blake asked.

She glanced up at her sister. "Yeah?"

"You okay? You look a little queasy."

"I'm fine. I think that piece of calzone that got stuck in my throat really took it out of me." She rose, wrapped up her calzone, and put it in the refrigerator. "Thanks for dinner. I think I'll save it for lunch tomorrow."

"Sure." Blake watched her carefully as if she were afraid Wanda was going to hack up another lung. Or maybe she was onto Wanda and knew she was upset about Cameron. She was a spirit witch after all. She had to have sensed Wanda's mood change.

Desperate to move on from thinking about Cameron, Wanda said, "I got you something today."

"You did? What?"

Wanda held up a finger, indicating Blake should wait for a moment, and then she disappeared into the living room. When she returned, she was holding a smartphone and handed it to Blake. "I got you this today."

Blake stared at it. When she finally looked up, she handed it back to Wanda. "Thanks, but I can't take this."

"Yes you can," Wanda insisted. "All you have right now is a burner phone. I'd rather you have one that has GPS and lets you download apps so you can join the twenty-first century. It wasn't expensive if that's the problem. I had a credit for an upgrade I don't need and it's a family plan, so the cost is reasonable." She shoved the phone at Blake again. "Think of this as a sacrifice to make your sister happy, all right?"

Blake shook her head, her expression pained.

"What is it, Blake?" Wanda asked, sitting down next to her. "It's just a phone."

"It's a new number," she said quietly and glanced away.

"Oh." Right. Her parents wouldn't know how to get in touch with her if she changed her number. Normally one would just text their contacts their new number, but Blake had already told Wanda that her mother's phone was no longer in service. Even though they'd abandoned her, Wanda completely understood wanting to have at least one avenue to possibly reconnect. "Well, there's no harm in keeping both for a little while, right? Just in case."

"Pay for two phones?" she asked, looking at Wanda as if she'd lost her mind.

"I'll pay for your new phone. That's what I planned to do anyway. You pay for your old one for however long you think you need to keep that number."

"That seems sort of unreasonable, doesn't it?" Blake's dark eyes glistened with tears. "It's stupid to think..." She shook her head again. "Never mind."

Wanda wrapped her arm around her sister and pulled her in for a sideways hug. "It's not stupid. Even if you don't want to talk to them ever again, I know this feels like cutting them off permanently since they'd have no idea how to get in touch with you unless they come looking for me. And we both know that's unlikely. So keep the phone on. You'll know when or if you're ready to give it up. There's no pressure there. Or judgment. You do what you need to."

Blake pressed her head against Wanda's shoulder and whispered, "Thank you for the phone... and everything."

"You're welcome, sis." Wanda kissed the top of her head. "Now, how about cupcakes?"

Blake pulled away. "You baked?"

"If only. I'd love to make some red velvet cupcakes, but who has time? I got some from A Spoonful of Magic. Shannon said they will rock our world."

Wanda got up from the table and retrieved a pastry box. While she was fishing the cupcakes out, her phone buzzed. Blake grabbed it and typed something out. "What are you doing?" Wanda asked.

"Nothing," she said with a laugh. "Just clearing this spam off your phone."

"Spam?" Wanda handed her a cupcake and took her phone. There wasn't any evidence of a text. She must've deleted it. "What did it say?"

"Something about sending a wire transfer to Siberia. I told them to lose your number. Then I blocked and deleted."

"Siberia?" Wanda raised a skeptical eyebrow. "Isn't it usually from a prince in Nigeria or something like that?"

"Prince? Well hell, if I'd known that, I would've asked for the wire instructions," she teased.

Wanda laughed, and felt her insides warm. She'd managed to cheer Blake up, and that was all that mattered.

Ten minutes later, when they were curled up on the couch scanning the channels for a movie, there was a knock on the door.

"That's my cue. Goodnight, Wanda." Blake waved her fingers at her sister and then ran up the stairs.

"Cue for what?" Wanda muttered as she opened the door.

"Hey." Cameron smiled down at her. His salt-and-pepper hair was unruly as if he'd run his hand through it a half dozen too many times, but his dark eyes were bright and dancing with joy.

"Cameron, um, what's going on?" She stepped back, letting him into the living room. She was so surprised by his visit she forgot she was mad at him, but as soon as she remembered what Blake said about his son, the fire ignited in her belly, and before he could say anything else, she said, "Just tell me one thing."

"Sure. Anything." He reached for her hand, but she jerked it away. The joy vanished from his gaze and was replaced by concern. "What's wrong?"

"*What's wrong?* You have a son. Cam, the kid I helped find an apartment and a job, is *your* son. You lied to me. But what I don't understand is, why? Do you have a wife or a girlfriend down in Los Angeles or something? Because otherwise, lying to me doesn't make any sense."

"Whoa. Calm down just a minute. I can—"

"Calm down? Did you just tell me to calm down? Don't tell me how to react to this. Lying is unforgivable. If you think—"

"Wanda!" he shouted. "Stop. I didn't lie to you. I swear."

"But—"

"I didn't know," he said more softly. "I just found out."

Wanda was stunned into silence. She stared at him, her mouth hanging open, and she felt like a complete idiot. It wasn't often she lost her cool. Obviously, Cameron got under her skin, otherwise she wouldn't have been ranting like a lunatic to someone she'd already cut loose. She closed her eyes and took a deep breath. *Son of a monkey*. She was in deep trouble with this one. *Friends*. Right.

"That was pretty much my exact reaction," he said with a chuckle. "Cam called me right before I left for Vancouver. He didn't know I was his father until he found his original birth certificate while going through his mother's things. She passed away six months ago, leaving no answers about her actions. We're all adjusting."

"You just found this out?" she asked, still trying to process what he'd said.

"Yes. I met him for the first time today at the café."

"Holy hell, and here I am giving you grief." All of her anger was gone, replaced by awe and compassion. Considering he'd just found out he had a grown son, Cameron seemed to be handling it better than she could even fathom.

"Just a little." He winked at her and then brought her hand up to his lips. He kissed her fingers and let out a contented sigh. "I missed these hands."

"I missed those lips," Wanda said and immediately regretted it. What was she doing? Just because he hadn't lied to her, it didn't mean she'd changed her mind about the status of their relationship. She still had Blake to think about, and he still lived in a different part of the state.

But his son lives here now, her not-so-helpful brain reminded her.

Cameron leaned in and brushed his lips over hers, sending a shiver of anticipation through her.

Wanda hadn't just been flirting. She really had missed his kisses. She missed *him*. All of her previous relationships had ended because they were mostly work and not worth the effort. But with Cameron, their time together was just easy. They didn't demand a lot from each other, and they respected each other's careers. Most men she'd dated had expected her to take a backseat to their wants and needs. Cameron hadn't ever made her feel that way. Why was she pushing him away again?

Right. *Blake.* Wanda didn't want her to get attached to someone who was going to walk away like everyone else in her life. There just wasn't any way of getting around the fact that Cameron lived and worked over six hundred miles away.

Wanda backed up, trying to put some space between them for her own sanity, and then retreated to the couch. Cameron followed and took a seat next to her. "So, how was it? Meeting Cam today? I helped him find his place. He seems like a good kid."

"He does, doesn't he?" Cameron smiled, looking like a proud papa.

Wanda hesitated for a moment but had to voice the questions in her mind. It's what she'd ask any friend in his position, so she blurted, "I do have to ask though, how do you know for sure you're his dad? If his mom never told him, how do you know she didn't lie on the birth certificate? There must be some reason why she never said anything."

"There's no question, Wanda," he said, shaking his head. "To be honest, I thought the same thing at first. But there's no mistaking his resemblance to my father. Cam looks exactly like a photo I have of Dad when he was twenty years old."

"Oh, wow. You must be so angry that she kept you in the dark." Wanda wanted to hunt the woman down and chew her a new one. But didn't he just say that she'd passed away recently? Damn. So much for her ass-kicking plans. Keeping a kid from a loving parent was wrong on so many levels.

"I have to admit, I'm furious at Tori," Cameron said. "What she did is unforgivable. But she must've been a great mother, because Cam is everything I'd ever want in a son. From what I've seen, he's kind, self-sufficient, humble, and determined. He's careful to stress that he doesn't want anything from me except to get to know me. Of course, I already want to do whatever I can to make his life easier. I offered money for school if he wants it, but he refused. Says he's not here for my money. For my part, I don't care if he goes to school. If he's happy doing construction, then that's what he should do. I just want him to have opportunities and not settle because of a lack of resources." Cameron chuckled. "I sound like I'm getting ahead of myself, don't I? I've known him one day, and I'm already turning into a helicopter dad."

Wanda snorted. "You're far from a helicopter dad. I think it's great that you want to support him. Far too many people have parents who just don't care."

"You know what's crazy?" he asked her.

"I'm sure there's a lot crazy about this situation," she said, scooting closer and resting her head on his shoulder. No matter how much she told herself to keep her distance, it was physically impossible. If he was near, she wanted to touch him.

"You've got that right." He wrapped an arm around her shoulders and pulled her in a little bit closer. "It's astounding how much I care. It's been less than a week since he called and spilled the news, and yet, I can't even imagine a reality now where Cam isn't in my life."

"It's like you've been sprinkled with magical father dust." She glanced up at him. "It isn't at all the same, but since Blake has been here, she's been my primary concern. My life has taken a major backseat to her needs, and I wouldn't have it any other way. Showing up for people is rewarding in its own way. But it's more than that, though. I feel like I have been entrusted with a piece of her heart and it's up to me to keep it whole."

"That's it exactly," Cameron said. "How did you do that?"

"Do what?"

"Put what I'm feeling into words."

She just smiled at him.

Cameron's gaze swept over her and then landed on her lips again. "Wanda, you're incredible."

Her insides warmed with pleasure, and she forgot all of her arguments for keeping him at arm's length.

"Let me take you on a date. No more pretending that we're just friends, or friends with benefits, or whatever. I want to date you."

Just like that, her happy bubble burst. Dating? Wasn't that a terrible idea? Even if she left Blake out of the equation, he'd just found out he was a father. "Are you sure that's a good idea? Don't you want to spend the time you have here in Keating Hollow getting to know your son? I wouldn't feel right about intruding on that."

"I can't spend every waking moment with him. He has a job. How about a lunch date? A day when he's working and Blake is in school. You have to eat, right? Even on your days at the office. Whatever you want. Woodlines for seafood? Or burgers at the brewery? Or if the weather is nice, how about a picnic down at the river? You could whip us up a fire, and I could bring the blanket."

Well, wasn't he charming? "You're too good to be true."

"Is that a yes?" he asked hopefully.

"Yes. But not tomorrow. I have too many appointments. Make it the next day and it's a date."

"You're on." Cameron dipped his head and gave her one more long, lingering kiss. Then he got up, mimed tipping his hat, and said goodnight.

Wanda wandered upstairs in a happy daze. She was just about to disappear into her room for the night when she heard a choked sob from Blake's bedroom. She froze. When she heard it again, she turned around and knocked softly. "Blake, honey. Are you all right?"

"I'm… fine," she said through another sob.

"You definitely do not sound fine. I'm coming in, okay?" When her sister didn't answer, Wanda knocked once and let herself into the room. Blake was curled up on her bed, her face puffy and eyes red from crying, and she was holding the smartphone Wanda had given her.

"I'm fine," she said with a sniffle.

"Oh, honey. No you're not." Wanda crawled right onto the bed with her and wrapped her arms around her sister from behind. "It's okay to not be okay. You know that, right?"

"I should be used to this by now," she said.

"Used to what?" Wanda smoothed her hair.

She took a deep breath. "I don't need the burner phone anymore."

Dread made Wanda uneasy. "Why?"

Blake didn't answer.

Wanda didn't want to push, so she just held her, waiting her out. When she was ready, she'd talk.

The pair laid together on the bed for so long without speaking that Wanda was pretty sure Blake had fallen asleep. But as soon as she started to uncurl from her sister, Blake said, "I messaged my new number to everyone in my contacts."

"And?" Wanda whispered.

"Mom texted me back, demanding to know where I got the money for a new phone. Apparently, she found a way to get her phone turned back on." Blake's tone was so heartbroken and dejected that for the second time that night, Wanda wanted to strangle another woman.

"Did you tell her I bought it?" Wanda asked.

"No. It's none of her business. She didn't care enough to say goodbye when she left or message me even once. And now she's concerned with what I'm doing? She's lucky I didn't block her."

"I know you're probably not ready, but it is okay to do that, you know. You do not have to open yourself up to her abuse. You're safe here. Always. Understand?"

Blake nodded, and a tiny bit of Wanda's tension eased. All she wanted was for her sister to feel safe and loved. That was enough.

CHAPTER 13

Cameron walked into the Enchanted K Gallery on Main Street. He was meeting his parents for dinner at their new rental property and didn't want to show up empty-handed. A bottle of wine would have been easier, but he knew his mother. She had a deep appreciation of handcrafted art. She'd love nothing more than to display something in her new home from a local artist.

The bell chimed, bringing with it the scent of the ocean, followed by a whiff of the redwoods. This was definitely his mother's kind of place. He imagined she'd spend a mint in the gallery in no time.

"Cameron, hey man. How's it going?"

Cameron turned and spotted Gideon Alexander, Miranda's significant other. He was busy arranging a display of redwood sculptures. Each of them had been carved and had a different scene of Keating Hollow burned into them. "Good. You?"

"Can't complain. Miranda's busy working on her new book, so I've been busy in the studio. And now that I have help with the remodel on the house I bought, everything is moving along nicely. That kid of yours is terrific."

Kid of yours. That was strange to hear, even as his heart felt like it was going to burst right out of his chest as it swelled with pride. It was going to take some time to get used to his new normal. "Can't tell you how good it is to hear that things are working out."

"Couldn't be happier." Gideon pulled a blue baseball cap out of the pocket of his faded blue jeans and stuffed it on his head, hiding his unruly, wavy hair that looked like it was about a month overdue for a cut. Cameron nearly laughed at the transformation of the man who not too long ago had been dressed and groomed with the polish of a Hollywood movie executive. His time in Keating Hollow had turned him into the laidback artist he was meant to be.

"What brings you in today?" Gideon asked.

"Looking for a housewarming present for my mom. She and my dad rented a house here to see if they're interested in making the move permanent. Can't show up for dinner empty-handed." Cameron glanced around the gallery, noting there wasn't a salesperson around, just Gideon. "Are you working here now? What's the owner's name? Ashe?"

"Yes, Ashe is the owner, but she's back in school," he said. "I've been helping out a few days a week while she's in class. Now, what are you looking for? A painting? Sculpture? Glass art?"

Cameron moved closer to the wood sculptures Gideon had been arranging. "Did you do these?"

"Yep. They're brand-new. You're the first one to see them other than Ashe and Miranda. But you haven't seen the best part yet." Gideon picked up one of the sculptures and ran his hand over the piece, magically lighting up the lampposts and the windows of Incantation Café.

"Whoa. That's impressive," Cameron said, admiring the never-ending fire he'd used to complete the effect. "Sold."

Gideon grinned. "I am rather pleased with the outcome of these. Do you want me to gift wrap it?"

"You gift wrap?" Cameron asked with a heavy dose of skepticism.

He chuckled. "Well, gift bag. But it gets the job done."

"Then wrap it up."

Once the sculpture was wrapped and paid for, Gideon handed it over and said, "Miranda tells me you've been seeing Wanda."

Just the sound of her name lit Cameron up inside. He hadn't been able to get her off his mind since he'd left her house the night before. If he'd had his way, he'd wouldn't have left until that morning, but he understood her position and resigned himself to being patient. "Yes, I guess we are."

"Good. The four of us should get together sometime."

The door opened, and in walked a petite blonde wearing a Keating Hollow Fire Department T-shirt that was at least two sized too big for her and jeans.

"Hey, Amelia. How's it going?" Gideon asked.

"Not bad. You?"

"Great. What can I get you?"

"Nothing. I'm here to check your fire extinguishers." She walked over to Cameron and held out her hand. "I don't think we've met. I'm Amelia Holiday, newest hire for the Keating Hollow Fire Department."

"Cameron Copeland. Writer. Nice to meet you."

She just nodded, seemingly unimpressed with his career of

choice. Cameron almost laughed. It was exactly what he loved about Keating Hollow. None of the locals were impressed with him. There was none of the pretentiousness of Hollywood, where everyone lived or died by the connections they made.

Amelia glanced at Gideon again. "I'll just take a look around and make sure everything is up-to-date. Is that all right?"

"Sure."

Amelia moved behind the counter and retrieved a fire extinguisher to check the dates.

Cameron was just about to take off when Amelia let out a gasp, ducked behind the counter, and said, "I'm not here. Whatever he says, I'm not here."

The door chimed again, and a tall man wearing black trousers and a black and white pinstriped button-down shirt walked in. Cameron glanced at the counter where Amelia remained hidden and then back at the man.

"Hi. I'm looking for Amelia Holiday. I was told she might be here. Have you seen her?" the guy asked, his voice thick with what sounded like a Boston accent.

"Amelia Holiday?" Gideon asked, furrowing his brow as if he were trying to decide if he knew an Amelia. "Nope. Haven't seen anyone other than Cameron here in a few hours. Sorry."

The man frowned. "The firehouse said this was a stop on her rounds today. Do you mind if I hang around for a bit?"

"I wish I could say yes," Gideon said seamlessly, "but my buddy Cameron here and I are just getting ready to head to lunch. The shop will be closed for the next hour or two."

Cameron nearly chuckled at how apologetic Gideon sounded. For a man who used to produce movies, he sure was one hell of an actor. He could've been just as successful in front of the camera as he was behind the scenes.

"But if I run into her, I can tell her you're looking for her if you'd like," Gideon added.

The man let out a frustrated sigh and said, "Thanks. Just tell her Grayson is looking for her. I'm staying at the Keating Hollow Inn."

"Sure thing, man," Gideon said with a nod.

Grayson walked out of the gallery, shoved his hands in his pockets, and with his head down, he strode down the street in the direction of the inn.

"He's gone," Cameron said.

"Are you sure?" Amelia asked.

"You do realize that if he was still here, he would've heard you, right?" Gideon teased.

She popped back up, staring wide-eyed at the front door. "What did he want?" she asked as if she hadn't heard every word he'd said.

"I'm guessing he wanted to talk to you," Gideon said. All of his humor fled, and concern flashed in his eyes. "Is there something here we should be worried about? Is this guy stalking you or something? Should we call Drew?"

"The deputy sheriff?" she squeaked. "Oh no. Nothing like that. Grayson is..." She squeezed her eyes shut. "We have history, and I'm just not ready to talk to him yet."

"Ah, I see." Gideon nodded at her. "Well, looks like he's here for a bit, so you're likely to run into each other sooner or later."

"Yeah. That's what I'm afraid of." She made a note on her clipboard and then said, "I'll come back later to finish my check. I think I need some time to figure out what to do."

Cameron watched her as she hurried out of the store. He

turned to Gideon, not quite convinced that Amelia had been telling the truth about Grayson. "What do you think? Is he dangerous?"

"It's hard to tell, but rest assured, I'll be letting Drew know to keep an eye on him."

Satisfied with that answer, Cameron asked for directions to the place Gideon was remodeling, and then took off to drop in on his son.

THE FARMHOUSE on Third Street sat near the river and had a separate garage. The property didn't look like it had been landscaped in a few years, but the white house had been freshly painted and had a gorgeous porch. Cameron had a twinge of regret that he hadn't found the place first.

Cam's VW bus was parked near the garage, confirming that his son was there. Cameron ran up the steps and knocked on the door. After a few beats, he tried again. When no one answered, Cameron headed toward the garage, assuming Cam was in his apartment. But before he got to the stairs, he heard a murmur of voices coming from the rear of the house.

He switched gears, assuming Cam had help that day and was working on the back of the house. But as soon as he rounded the corner, he spotted Cam hugging Blake while she buried her head in his shoulder.

Feeling awkward and knowing he'd just walked in on a private moment, he retreated back around the house and then called out, "Cam? Are you back here?"

By the time he rounded the corner again, Cam and Blake had broken apart, but Cameron didn't miss the way Cam was clutching Blake's hand. Were they dating? Hadn't they just met? If they were, that was fast. But then who was Cameron to talk? It wasn't like it took very long for him and Wanda to fall into bed together. That thought brought a whole new set of worries when it came to the pair of teenagers. *Please don't let them be sleeping together already.* That was something neither he nor Wanda needed to be worrying about.

"Hey, Cameron," Cam said. "Were you looking for me?"

"Sure was." He pasted on a smile and climbed up on the back deck. There was no mistaking the fact that Blake had been crying. He frowned as he studied her red, swollen eyes. "Are you okay, sweetheart?"

"I'm fine." She sniffled and pulled her hand away from Cam's to wipe at her eyes. It was then he noticed she was holding a stack of bills in her other hand. When she saw him eyeing the cash, she quickly stuffed it into her jeans pocket. "Just some allergies."

Cameron was tactful enough to not point out that it wasn't exactly allergy season yet. Clearly, she was upset and Cam had been comforting her. But it was also clear she wasn't going to be sharing whatever it was that had made her upset. "Yeah. Allergies are the worst."

He got to the point of his visit. "Cam, I actually came by to invite you to dinner with my parents. Mom is cooking. And trust me when I say you don't want to miss that."

Cam blinked a few times, clearly processing the invitation. Then he said, "I'd love to meet my grandparents, but…" He looked at Blake again and added, "Can we do it another time? We had plans to hang out tonight."

"No! You should go," Blake insisted. "Don't worry about me. I'll be fine."

"It's no big deal," Cam said and squeezed her hand. "I can meet them later this week or over the weekend."

Blake shook her head. "I insist. Go meet them and then call me and tell me how wonderful they are."

He chuckled. "What if they're monsters and want me to join some crazy cult that sells flowers at airports?"

It was Cameron's turn to laugh. "Not likely. Your grandmother would definitely tease you about maybe living on a commune, but cult is a four-letter dirty word in her world. She's all about following your own path as long as you love the journey. I'm fairly positive she was big in the hippie movement back in the day."

"Now that *is* cool." He grinned at Cameron. "I'll be there. Just text me the time and the address."

Cameron walked away from them, both amused and worried. Wasn't Blake supposed to be in school? It was only two in the afternoon. Back in his day, high school never got out that early. He needed to call Wanda. Except he wasn't sure what he'd say. Was he going to tell her that Blake had skipped at least part of school or that she was upset and carrying an unreasonable amount of cash in her pocket?

The latter. Definitely. There was no need to cause a rift between them just because Blake missed a few hours of school. However, he couldn't ignore what he saw. Wanda needed to know something was up with her sister.

Cameron just hoped she wasn't the kind of woman to shoot the messenger. It was really going to be hard to take her out for that date if he ended up worm food.

CHAPTER 14

Cameron pulled his SUV to a stop in the driveway of the gorgeous home that was embedded into the side of the mountain. Wanda had done a superb job of finding his parents a rental. It had taken calling a dozen or so owners who had vacation property in Keating Hollow and a lot of begging, but she'd done it. And his parents were thrilled. Not only did they have a view of the valley, there was also one of the enchanted river.

Just as he hopped out, he heard the sputtering sound of the VW bus climbing the hill. It didn't take long for the vehicle to appear. He waited for Cam to join him in front of the house and grinned when he spotted a wooden bird feeder in Cam's hands. "Did you make that?"

"Yes." Cam held it up, scrutinizing it. "Do you think your mom will like it?"

"She's going to love it." Cameron chuckled. "Damn, you're going to be her favorite. I bought my housewarming gift."

He laughed. "I need a head start after all these years."

Cameron sobered. "No, you don't. You just need to be here."

His son opened his mouth to reply, but before he could say anything, the front door opened and Emily ran outside wearing gray slacks, a white silk shirt, and a hot pink apron. Without a word to Cameron, she ran down the steps and flung her arms around Cam. "I can't believe it. A grandson. And you're here."

Cam wrapped his arms around his grandmother while Cameron watched them. Warmth spread through his body, and he couldn't remember a time when he'd felt so… complete.

"Hey, son," Dayton Copeland said as he stepped out onto the front porch. As usual, his dad was wearing jeans and a short-sleeved button-down shirt. He'd dressed his look up with a fedora for the evening though, making Cameron chuckle. That was one way to hide the fact that he was balding. "Looks like you found me a mini-me."

Cameron nodded and moved up onto the porch. "The genes are strong with this one."

"Emily, are you going to let that nice young man go?" Dayton draped an arm around Cameron's shoulders as he watched his wife in amusement.

"No," she called, still clinging to Cam. "I missed out on nineteen years of hugs. I'll let him go sometime around Tuesday."

Cam had placed his bird feeder on the ground and was hanging onto Emily just as tightly as she was on to him. The kid's eyes were closed, but Cameron was certain he saw a single tear roll down his cheek. The scene was so emotionally charged that Cameron had to fight to keep from getting choked up.

"All right," Dayton said. "You two can stay out here if you like, but Cameron and I are going to go in and check on the lasagna. We don't want the cheese to burn again."

"The lasagna!" Emily jumped back, releasing Cam. "I'm on it. Need to check the bread, too." She ran back in the house, leaving the men chuckling.

Dayton strode off the porch and held his hand out to Cam. "I'm Dayton. Your grandfather."

"Hi." Cam took his hand in his and then was swept up in another hug by his grandfather, only he didn't hold Cam captive quite so long.

When Dayton pulled back, he stared at his doppelgänger and let out a low whistle. "Cameron wasn't kidding when he said the resemblance is uncanny. It's just like looking in a mirror when I was your age."

"Really?" Cam's lips curved into a smile. "So this is what I'm going to look like thirty years from now?"

Dayton laughed. "More like forty, kid, but points for trying to make an old man feel good about himself."

Cameron rolled his eyes. "You're not old. You're not even sixty yet."

"Close enough." He chuckled and jerked his head toward the house. "Come on, kid. I hope you're not a vegan because your grandmother's lasagna is a meat lover's paradise."

"I'm not, and lasagna sounds amazing." He picked up his bird feeder and followed them into the tastefully decorated cottage.

The place wasn't overly big, but whoever had built it hadn't spared any expense. From the built-ins in the living room to the marble counters in the kitchen to the floor-to-ceiling windows, Cameron couldn't think of anything he'd change if he owned the house. It was perfect for his parents.

"Is this where you're staying while you're in town?" Cam asked his father.

"Yeah." Cameron nodded and placed his gift bag on the kitchen island. "There's a guest room downstairs where I can hold my wild parties," he teased.

"Just keep the noise down, dear," his mother called as she retrieved the garlic bread from the oven.

"Don't worry. We'll be sure to play Fleetwood Mac. That way you won't care how loud it is," Cameron said and moved into the kitchen to grab some sodas from the refrigerator.

"I do love Stevie Nicks." Emily bustled around the kitchen, humming "Rhiannon" to herself.

Cameron passed a can of soda to Cam and then got busy in the kitchen helping his mom get dinner on the table. When the lasagna was in place, salads served, and the bread tucked into a basket, Emily clasped her hands together and said, "I think we're ready."

"Wait," Cameron said. "Presents first."

"But the lasagna," Emily said, eyeing the dish.

"It's not going anywhere." He grabbed the gift bag Gideon had given him and handed it over. "A housewarming gift."

She beamed at him. "Cameron, you did *not* have to do this. It's not like this is our permanent home."

"It is for the time being. Besides, I know you'll want to take this with you when you leave."

Dayton leaned against the counter, watching with an amused smile. He turned to Cameron. "Just because you brought her something doesn't mean you're getting the biggest piece of tiramisu. You know that, right?"

Cameron crossed his arms over his chest. "We'll see." His mother always gave his father the biggest piece of dessert because she said it was her way of letting him know she was still sweet on him. It had been a running joke in the family that someday Cameron was going to figure out a way to earn the bigger share. So far, he'd been unsuccessful. Although Emily claimed he'd come close the time he'd surprised her with tickets to *Hamilton*.

"Are you two never going to let that—" Emily stopped mid-sentence and gasped out loud when she saw the wood sculpture. "Oh, wow, Cameron. This is... It's incredible. Where did you get it?"

"The Enchanted K Gallery. Gideon was just putting them on display when I stopped in there today."

"It's exquisite. The details of the town, the lighting. I can't get over it." When she finally glanced at her son, there were happy tears shining in her eyes.

He held his arms out, already knowing she was going to demand a hug. Once she was in his arms, she whispered, "I'll put an extra piece of tiramisu in your to-go bag. This definitely calls for the bigger share of dessert."

"Thanks, Mom," he whispered back and kissed the top of her head.

She pulled back and carefully wiped at her eyes so that she didn't smear her makeup. "So... dinner?"

"Cam has something for you, too," Cameron said.

"You do?" she asked, turning to her grandson. "You didn't need to bring anything. Your presence is more than enough."

"It was no big deal." Cam reached for the birdfeeder. He'd placed it in the seat of one of the chairs, just to make sure it was out of the way. "I made this in my spare time. Gideon helped with the lettering. I hope you like it."

Emily's eyes widened in surprise when she spotted the birdfeeder. It was clear she hadn't noticed it earlier when she'd come flying out of the house and tackle-hugged him.

"It's not much, but I thought if you like birds then—"

"It's lovely, Cam," she said reverently. "Just lovely." The house was a basic square, but it had cutouts in the shapes of birds that could have only been done by a practiced hand. *Welcome to the Copelands* had been burned into the back with a tiny, thin red line glowing like embers in all of the grooves of the letters. "Gideon helped me with that lettering. I'm a spirit witch, so I don't have the ability to manipulate fire like that."

"Gideon has proven to be quite the talented artist, hasn't he?" Emily mused, looking at her two gifts. "But he doesn't hold a candle to my two boys. So thoughtful. What did I do to deserve you both?"

"You're an angel from above," Dayton said and kissed his wife on the cheek. "Now, let's eat before this wonderful meal gets cold."

The four of them sat down to dinner. All throughout the meal, Emily had trouble keeping her emotions under control. When Cam told a story about picking out a puppy as a kid, she cried. When he told them about his best friend who recently moved to Hawaii to try to make it as a professional surfer, she cried. And when he told them about the girl he'd asked out in first grade, she cried.

"I'm sorry," she said, sniffling and dabbing her eyes with a tissue Dayton had retrieved for her. "There's just so much we missed. I would've loved to have been a part of your life."

"He's here with us now, sweetheart," Dayton said, patting her hand.

She smiled through her tears. "I know. And I'm so grateful. Just emotional."

Cameron was right there with her. As his son was telling his stories, he couldn't help but think about Tori and get angry all over again. What exactly had he done that had been so awful that she'd kept Cam away from him? It couldn't have been too terrible since she'd named him Cam. It just didn't make any sense, and it burned him up inside that he wouldn't ever have the chance to demand answers.

Emily reached over and clasped her hand over Cam's. "I just want you to know that we are so grateful that you're here now, and I'm trying my best to remember that your mother must've had her reasons. A mother always does."

Anger bubbled up from the depths of Cameron's soul. He was glad his mother was finding a way to forgive, but he seriously doubted he ever would. She'd taken memories from him that he'd never get back. "What kind of reason would be good enough to keep me from my father and my grandparents?" Cam asked, staring at his half-finished meal.

"Well, I…" Emily placed a hand to her throat and looked at Cameron as if he might have the answer.

Cameron shrugged. "Don't ask me. I've been pondering that same question for a week now. The only answer I can come up with is maybe she thought I'd be a terrible father."

"You? Terrible?" His mother scoffed. "Hardly. I've never met a man more suited for parenthood."

"You're bias," Cameron said with a laugh. "But thanks for the vote of confidence."

"I don't think that was it," Dayton said. "Why would she have named Cam after you or even put your name on the birth certificate if she thought so poorly of you?"

Cam blew out a frustrated breath. "I'll be honest. After meeting you, I'm having to try really hard to forgive my mother. Until we met, I guess I thought she might've had a good reason to not say anything, but what could that possibly be? Cameron wanted to marry her. You two… Well, you seem like dream grandparents. Instead, I got a single mother whose longest relationship was about three years before she kicked her out."

"Her?" Cameron raised one eyebrow.

Cam grimaced to himself and then lifted his gaze, staring Cameron right in the eye. "Yeah. Her name was Jessie, and she lived with us. She was great, too. Mom broke it off with her when I was seven, or maybe eight? After that, Mom's relationships never lasted more than six months. But on the plus side, none of her boyfriends ever moved in either. I always wondered what happened with Jessie. I came home from school one day and she was just gone. I later got a birthday card that said she missed me, but that was it."

Cameron was surprised to hear that Tori had once had a girlfriend. He hadn't known that she wasn't strictly heterosexual, but he supposed it wasn't really out of character. Tori had been a curious and adventurous creature. "I'm sorry, Cam. You're too young to have lost so many people who were important to you."

"Oh, honey," Emily said to Cam. "If you're up to it, I think you should try to contact Jessie."

"Why?" he asked, looking defiant. It was a strange expression on him. Cameron couldn't help but marvel about how quickly Cam could flip from the boy next door to a young man with a chip on his shoulder.

Emily frowned. "Considering your mother kept you from Cameron, I think it's possible she might have blocked Jessie from seeing you, too. Plus, your mom might have talked to her about why she never told you about your dad."

Cam's eyes widened with surprise. "You know what, I hadn't considered either of those things. Mom never even talked about Jessie after she left. She just said she was gone and wouldn't be coming back. I don't even think I told her when I found the card in the mailbox because she never wanted to talk about her."

"Do you think there's a way to find her?" Emily asked.

"Not sure. I'll try an internet search and see if she's on any social media."

Cameron decided that the best thing for him to do was to keep his mouth shut about Tori. As angry as he was about the situation, he didn't want to be the one who stoked the flames and caused even more animosity toward her. Cam had a right to be upset, but hopefully if he found some answers, maybe he could make peace with the situation. Maybe they both could.

He'd left Tori behind a long time ago. In fact, when he thought of her, he always associated her with failure. He'd wanted to marry her, and despite all the love he'd had for her, she'd just walked away. The relationship had been a devastating failure, and he'd promised himself he'd never fall for a woman like that again. Never fail someone so completely again. Because surely if he'd been good enough, she would've stayed, right?

But as he took in everything Cam said about his mother, it became clear that Tori was the one who'd thrown it all away. Cameron hadn't been the failure at all. Tori was the one who couldn't maintain a relationship, for whatever reason, and the way she dealt with them was to completely disengage. She'd been the one to walk away. To make a clean break and then pretend the other person never existed.

Cameron had never been that type of person. He didn't just drop people. He was the type who stuck around. A true friend was precious and rare, and Cameron knew it. It was why he kept coming back to Keating Hollow. Miranda,

Wanda, Gideon, they were all people he intended to keep in his life. Especially Wanda.

Only Wanda wasn't just a friend. No. He wanted more with Wanda. He wanted everything with her. Finally, after twenty years, he was ready to lay it all on the line and take the risk he'd thought he'd never take again. He just had to figure out how to get her to take the same risk.

CHAPTER 15

"How was dinner with your parents last night?" Wanda asked Cameron as she buttered a piece of sourdough bread. They were at Woodlines, one of the fine dining restaurants on Main Street, and they mostly had the place to themselves. Since it was early February, there weren't many tourists in town, and most of the locals frequented the Townsends' brewpub for lunch.

"It was great, actually. My mother has promoted Cam to the favorite in the family, so I'm feeling a tiny bit slighted," he said with a laugh. "But who can blame her? He's a great kid."

"He does seem like a great kid," Wanda agreed. "Blake sure does seem to like him, too. It seems like all she does is talk to him when she isn't at school or working. Do you think that's moving too fast? They just met."

"Not really," Cameron said a little hesitantly. "They seem to have a connection. Cam told me last night that Blake's a spirit witch, too. I think that's part of it. He said she's the first person since his mom died that just seems to get him."

"That makes sense," Wanda said, nodding. "They have

other things in common, too. I guess it's good they have each other to lean on when things get hard."

Cameron studied her for a moment, and then he leaned forward and said, "Listen, Wanda. This is probably nothing, but I think I'd better tell you just in case it isn't."

Her smile vanished as she furrowed her brows. "What's nothing? Does it have to do with Blake?"

"Blake and Cam actually. I know Blake is almost an adult, and there's no doubt Cam already is, so this feels like an invasion of privacy or something, but—"

"But what? Stop with the build-up. You're making me nervous. Just spit it out, okay?"

"Yesterday afternoon, I went out to Gideon's place to talk to Cam, and when I got there, Blake was crying. Cam was holding her, comforting her, actually. So it didn't appear to be because there was anything wrong between them. And that's why I'm telling you instead of assuming it was just regular teenage drama. If something serious is wrong, I thought you should know."

Wanda's heart ached for her sister. Was this about her parents again? "I assume you asked what was wrong and she said she was fine?"

He gave her a sympathetic smile. "Pretty much verbatim."

"I've heard that one before, too," Wanda said with a sigh. "It's probably about her parents. They're being assholes as usual. Maybe I should try to get her some counseling. Her relationship with the two people who are supposed to love her most and keep her safe is completely dysfunctional. If I were her, I'd be a mess, too."

Cameron nodded. "Yes. It's hard to imagine. My parents are the poster children for what parenting should look like. Even though they are heartbroken they didn't get to watch

Cam grow up, they are already finding ways to forgive Tori while smothering Cam with so much love that he is probably wondering what he got himself into."

"I'm sure he loves it," Wanda said, shaking her head in amusement. But as she watched the light fade from Cameron's eyes, her smile vanished. "What about you? How are you dealing with this?"

He shrugged one shoulder. "Fine."

"Just fine?" she probed. He didn't look fine. In fact, he was starting to look murderous.

"Good."

She shook her head and let out a humorless laugh. "No, you aren't. Spill it. What's going on in that head of yours?"

"Seriously, I'm just really grateful that Cam found me. I don't know how it's possible to go from thinking it was best if I didn't ever have kids to…" He waved a hand in the air. "To being a proud father who wants nothing more than to spend some quality time with his son, all in a week's time."

A spark of joy had lit his eyes when he spoke of Cam, but it flickered out just as fast, and his features became stormy and full of tension.

Wanda reached across the table and took Cameron's hand. "I'm sure that's true, that you're happy about learning you have a son, but I'm also sure it's a crazy transition for you. It's one thing to think about kids in the abstract. It's another thing entirely when they show up on your doorstep out of the blue. I know it's not the same thing since Blake is my sister, but the responsibility I feel for that girl is unlike anything I've ever known. She's my only sister and needs someone to love her. I'm that person. It's both overwhelming and incredible to have someone need me that way. I can imagine you feel the same, only a hundred times more intensely since he's yours and he's been kept from you."

Cameron held her gaze, looking at her in a way that made her feel completely exposed. There was no other word for the expression on his face. It was full of pure awe.

"Stop," she said, staring at the salad the waiter had just put down in front of her.

"Stop what?" he asked.

"Looking at me like that."

"Like what?"

She let out a huff of irritation. "Like you're going to make me your goddess or something. I didn't say anything special. I was just calling it like I see it."

His gaze lowered to her lips, and his voice turned husky as he said, "You *are* a freakin' goddess, Wanda. And I'd love to show you just how I'd worship you."

Her face flushed with heat, and there was no question that she was blushing up a storm. But they were out for lunch, not a booty call. "Let's finish our meal, and then we'll get to the part about whether I'll let you worship me, all right?"

"Oh, you will," he said with an air of confidence that made her toes curl.

Son of a monkey. He'd gone there. She had to admit, she wouldn't mind a little bedroom worshiping, but not until she got to the bottom of what was bothering him. Because even though he was flirting shamelessly, he still had an air of frustration clinging to him no matter how hard he tried to hide it. She tilted her head and gave him a sexy half smile. "We'll see."

He winked and turned his attention back to his salad. It

wasn't long before he was jabbing the lettuce as if he were trying to punish it.

Wanda placed her fork down, pushed her salad away, and then folded her arms on the table as she leaned in and whispered, "You can tell me what's on your mind, you know. Come on, do it for the lettuce before you pulverize what's left on your plate."

"What are you going on about?" he asked, actually chuckling this time.

"Your lettuce. You're punishing it." She smiled at him. "It doesn't deserve that, does it?"

He stared down at his plate and then shook his head in disbelief. "I really did a number on it, didn't I?"

"Yep."

"Fine. I'll tell you," he said. "I'm trying really hard to find acceptance about losing nineteen years with Cam, but no matter what I tell myself or what mantra I try, I can't shake the all-consuming rage that is threatening to eat me up inside. There's no one to blame and no way to seek an explanation. I'm not only furious with Tori for keeping this secret, I'm also angry at her for dying and taking her secrets with her."

Wanda reached across the table and pressed her palm to his cheek. "Cameron, I think your emotions are not only valid, but reasonable, too. Honestly, I was starting to wonder how it was even possible for you to be so *normal*. Nothing about this situation is normal. It's a huge upheaval and you're doing great, but you also have to make space to deal with your feelings, own them, experience them. Only then will you be able to really and truly let them go. Just because you *want* to be the bigger man by forgiving Tori, it doesn't mean you're ready for that."

He closed his eyes and let out a breath. "Thanks. I needed that."

"You're welcome." She lowered her hand and slipped it into his. Squeezing, she said, "Now, tell me what else you're feeling. I can't be the only one who is all over the place. One minute I'm overjoyed at Blake being here, and the next I'm terrified. I mean, what do I know about being a guardian? How do I deal with it if she starts having sex? Or does drugs? Both of her parents are addicts. Or worse…" Wanda widened her eyes and pretended to be horrified. "What if she decides to try out for *cheerleading*?"

Cameron laughed. "Wanda Danvers. Did you just imply that there is something wrong with cheerleading?"

"Yes," she said, hanging her head and pretending to be ashamed. "But in my defense, it's completely irrational and based on the fact that I tried out and did not make the squad. They said my voice was too shrill."

"Shrill?" He pressed his lips together and shook his head, indicating he did not agree in any way with Suzy Francis in her assessment of Wanda's cheering voice. "Who do I need to hunt down and force to give you a new tryout?"

Wanda threw her head back and laughed. "I love that you sound completely serious right now. How about I just send an email to Suzy and inform her that her poor decisions will result in having her reunion invitation revoked."

"That sounds perfectly evil," Cameron agreed. "Any girl who cut another for her shrill voice probably remembers her high school years as the golden years. Withholding access is the best revenge."

"I'm glad you see it my way," Wanda said, chuckling. "Now, how about you? How are you really holding up this week?"

His lips curved into a genuine smile, and for the first time that afternoon, Wanda was finally convinced he wasn't hiding anything. "I'm completely out of my comfort zone. Terrified I'll really mess something up. Excited that I get to claim that wonderful kid as mine. And grateful to have the support of someone as amazing as you."

Cameron brushed her hair out of her eyes then leaned in and kissed her. Really kissed her. Wanda's entire body tingled with anticipation, only this time it wasn't just pure desire. Something had shifted between them. Cameron had opened up and shared a piece of his heart and in turn had taken a piece of hers. No matter what she told herself, they weren't just friends. They were definitely more. The only problem was that she wasn't sure how to label it or if she was ready for it. All she really knew for sure was that she was happy to be with him in that moment and wasn't going to waste a single minute second-guessing herself.

Wanda smiled at him and returned his kiss with everything she had.

CHAPTER 16

As far as Cameron was concerned, Wanda was an angel. He didn't know how, but she'd somehow managed to not only calm him down but to also validate his feelings and make him realize he wasn't crazy.

They'd finished their lunch and then shared a slice of caramel chocolate cheesecake. Cameron had a few bites, but then he'd been content to watch her eat the rest. It was the way she enjoyed it that got him. The murmurs of appreciation, her eyes rolling to the back of her head, and the way she kept licking her lips were all like a shot of pure testosterone.

The only thing he wanted to do was take her back to his room at the inn and spend the rest of the afternoon with her in bed. Except… ugh. He'd already checked out of his room, and he guessed renting a room by the hour wasn't going to fly with Noel.

"You're doing it again," she said mildly as they strolled down Main Street. Wanda had wanted to stretch her legs after sitting for so long at the restaurant.

"Doing what?"

"Looking at me like you want to eat me."

Cameron placed his palm on the small of her back, leaned in, and whispered, "I can't help it. I've been having Wanda withdrawals."

"Is that right?" she asked in that husky tone she always got when she was picking up what he was putting down.

"That's right." They strolled by the Keating Hollow Inn, and Cameron said, "If I still had my room there, I'd already have you inside and undressed."

"You gave up your room?" Wanda looked aghast at the idea and grimaced. "Are you really staying with your parents?"

"It's not as bad as you think," he said, tucking her closer to him as the wind picked up. "I have my own space downstairs and a separate entrance, but that doesn't mean I'd be comfortable bringing you back there. Some things should always remain private."

"You mean like when your parents walked in on me in nothing but a see-through negligée?"

Cameron groaned. "Do. Not. Remind. Me. I haven't been able to stop thinking about what I would've done if they hadn't been there. Goddess, Wanda. That was hot."

Wanda waved at Noel through the front window of the inn and ducked her head against the wind. When they reached A Spoonful of Magic, Wanda stopped and stared in the display case at the dancing chocolate-covered heart-shaped cookies. They were lined up in a chorus line with two cookies out front, gliding along together in what was no doubt meant to be a romantic night on the town.

"I want to be one of those cookies," Wanda said. "Lots of romance and lots of options."

"Options?" Cameron asked, raising his eyebrows. "I kinda thought you liked this option." He pointed to himself and eyed her until she answered.

"Of course I like that option. I just want to be romanced and learn exactly what it was you wanted to do when you saw me in that nightie," she said, jabbing lightly at his stomach. "Now, let's stop talking about cookies so you can take me back to my place and wow me with whatever it is you have up your sleeve."

Cameron stopped dead in his tracks and stared at her. "Did you just tell me to take you back to your place for an afternoon booty call?"

"It's not a booty call if it's a date," she said. "Now hurry up before I change my mind."

"You don't have to tell me twice." Cameron whisked her back to the SUV he'd rented, and once he was behind the wheel, he made record time back to Wanda's house.

WANDA CURLED into Cameron's arms and laid her head on his shoulder. They'd been back at her place for just over an hour, and she knew they'd have to get up soon before Blake came home, but she couldn't bring herself to break the spell just yet.

When they'd gotten to her house, they'd raced up the stairs, leaving clothes in their wake. It had been far too long since they'd been together, and it showed. They'd been frenzied, desperate for each other's touch. But soon, Cameron's kisses became slow and languid as if he was savoring every single second with her. It was tender and sweet and then full of raw passion.

He had been everything she'd ever dreamed of in a lover, and she wanted to hang onto it for just a few more minutes.

"You're incredible," Cameron whispered, stroking her bare arm with his fingertips.

"That's what you always say," she said sleepily. If only they could curl up and take a nap, then the day would be perfect.

"It's true. Every time we're together, I can't help but wonder what I did to deserve such a gorgeous, generous woman in my arms."

"Stop flattering me," she said with a laugh as she looked up at him. "You'll make me think this is something more than what it is."

Those dark eyes of his flashed with something she couldn't quite make out. But when he gently extracted himself from her arms and climbed out of the bed to start jerking his pants on, she recognized the look as frustration.

"Okay. What is it? What happened here just now." She scooted up on the bed and pressed the blanket to her chest, suddenly feeling the need to be covered.

"It's nothing," he said, shaking his head and reaching for his shirt.

"The hell it isn't," she said hotly. Their lovemaking had been just that. Making love. It wasn't something two people could fake. The tenderness. The generosity. The total body worshipping. All of those things combined meant that, whatever they had, it was a hell of a lot more than sleeping together. "Two seconds ago, we were lying here in post-coital bliss, and suddenly you're jumping out of bed and stuffing yourself back into your clothes as if this were a Tinder date and all you were here for was a quick lay."

"Isn't that what you wanted?" he asked, his tone carefully neutral. "For me to go before Blake gets home?"

Yes. That was what she wanted because she didn't want to add anything to Blake's life that might make it harder. And dating Cameron complicated things. But still, she wasn't exactly kicking him out of her bed. "It's true that I think it's better if you leave before she gets here, but it isn't true that I treated this like some random hookup. You know I like you. More than I should, probably. But that doesn't change the fact that we both have teenagers who are new to Keating Hollow. Don't you want the focus to be on Cam and Blake? Make sure they are adjusting to the changes in their lives before giving them something else to deal with?"

Cam studied her from his place near the bedroom door. He crossed his arms over his chest and let out a long sigh. "See, Wanda. That's where we're different on this subject. You think there's zero chance we'd make it as a couple. We're barely getting started, and you already see us ending. But me? I think that if you let yourself enjoy what we have, without worrying so much about how Blake will handle things, that we have a better than decent chance of being together forever."

"Forever?" Wanda felt the blood drain out of her face.

"What's wrong with forever?" Cameron asked her.

"I—um—we haven't known each other that long," she insisted, suddenly panicked at the thought that her "friend" was getting fed up with their arrangement. She wasn't ready to lose Cameron. But she also wasn't ready for a serious commitment.

"We've known each other for weeks, not days," he countered. When she didn't respond, he gave her a curt nod. "I understand, Wanda. But don't expect me to do this again. I think we both know there's more here than just desire. Let me know when you're ready to do something about it."

Wanda watched as he walked out of her room and straight to the stairs. Her front door slammed with a finality that told her he wasn't coming back. At least not today.

CHAPTER 17

Wanda was still reeling from the blow up with Cameron. What exactly had happened? They'd had a wonderful lunch and a walk that led directly to a seriously fantastic afternoon in bed. And then, Cameron freaked out. All because he clearly wanted more from their relationship and she was hesitant. She'd thought that they were both on the same page. Casual. Nothing too serious. That's what they'd been before Blake and Cam showed up.

Sure they were getting closer, and she could see how her flippant comment about their relationship not being more than what it was could push the wrong buttons. But didn't it make more sense to be cautious now that their lives had changed significantly?

Rushing into a relationship had never been Wanda's MO. Prior to their argument, she'd been certain it wasn't Cameron's either. As far as she knew, he'd never had a serious relationship after Tori left him twenty years ago. Did he somehow think that now that he had a son that he needed the wife and dog, too?

She climbed out of bed and stomped into the shower. She didn't need this grief. Blake would be home soon, and Wanda didn't want to spend the evening pissed off about Cameron's temper tantrum because she hadn't professed her undying love.

Her heart started to ache.

Love.

Was she in love with him? Her stomach flipped, and her heart sped up as she thought of him. What would she do if he decided she wasn't worth waiting for? That ache throbbed in her chest again. Would she be able to stay away from him?

No. She wouldn't.

And what if he took up with someone new? Someone like Amelia Holiday, maybe. She was new in town and really pretty. Why wouldn't Cameron be interested in someone like her?

"Stop it," Wanda ordered herself as the hot water sluiced over her. Nothing good was going to come from speculating about what-ifs. She just needed to calm down, let her thoughts settle, and then she'd talk to Cameron tomorrow after they both had time to regroup.

Freshly showered and dressed in yoga pants and a sweatshirt, Wanda made her way down to the kitchen, where she got to work on cooking dinner. Over the years of cooking for one, she'd gotten into quite the rut of what she ate, but now that Blake was around, Wanda had started trying new recipes. Tonight's experiment was ceviche bowls with tortilla and avocado.

Wanda was halfway through cutting up her sushi grade tuna when her phone buzzed with an incoming text. Not wanting to interrupt her chopping, she waited until she had all of her fish cubed and transferred into the marinade before she washed her hands and went to retrieve the message.

Blake: *School was fine. Nothing interesting to report. Just wanted to let you know I won't be home for dinner. Cam is taking me to dinner on the coast.*

Wanda frowned. It was a school night. Catching dinner with Cam in town was one thing. But heading all the way out to the coast? That was an hour and a half round trip of travel alone. She tapped out a reply. *Why the coast? It's a school night. Wouldn't it be easier to just have dinner at the Cozy Cave or Woodlines?*

Blake: *Don't worry. I'll be home before 10.*

Ten was still late for a school night. What if she had homework? Wanda almost texted back asking her about it but forced herself to put her phone down. She'd been a guardian for less than two weeks, and already she was fighting her urge to hover. Goddess above. How did parents get through the teenage years?

Blake was seventeen. Almost eighteen. And responsible. If she wanted to make a run over to the coast with Cam, Wanda wasn't going to stop her. But if her schoolwork suffered or she was dead on her feet the next day, that was a lesson she'd have to learn.

Wanda: *Thanks for letting me know.*

Blake: *You should go out, too. Why don't you give Cameron a call? Have some adult fun for a change?*

She'd already done that, and look at where it had gotten her. Wanda ignored Blake's suggestion and texted back: *Be safe.*

Blake replied with a heart emoji, indicating that the conversation was over.

Wanda glanced over at her ceviche bowl and sighed. The

thought of eating by herself that night after the fight she'd had with Cameron was just too much. The unfamiliar pangs of loneliness started to creep in, and she hated it. Wanda was never lonely. In fact, she was usually the life of the party.

She had to get out of her house, or she was going to lose it. She tapped Abby's name in her contacts.

"Hey, girl," Abby said after the first ring. "What's up?"

"Are you busy tonight?"

"I had big plans of sitting on my butt and watching the *Kitchen Witch,* but if you have something else in mind, I'm game. Olive is working on a school project at her friend Ashley's house and Clay is working, so I'm available."

"Can you meet me at Incantation Café in twenty minutes?" Wanda was suddenly dying for a latte and one of Hanna's double chocolate cupcakes.

"I'm all yours," Abby said.

"Bring your golf cart. It's a racing night." Wanda ended the call, put her ceviche away in the refrigerator, and then ran upstairs to change into something a little warmer. The weather had been mild, but it was still a February evening in Keating Hollow. Yoga pants weren't going to cut it.

"NICE FIRE," Abby said twenty-five minutes later when she parked her magically enhanced golf cart right next to Wanda's.

"You like that?" She glanced over at the self-contained fire, crackling away in the parking spot on her left-hand side. "I needed something to keep me warm while I waited outside for your tardy butt."

"I'm only five minutes late," Abby insisted. She climbed

out of her cart and pressed her hands to her lower back as she arched backward, stretching.

"On mommy time already." Wanda winked at her and passed her a cup of hot chocolate. "This is for you because I love you so much."

"Oh. Em. Gee," Abby said, taking a sip. "You're a goddess."

"I know. Now, do you want to be on my team, or do you want to go head to head and pick teams from the lineup?" Wanda slid out of her cart and headed toward the front door of Incantation Café.

"Um, what?" Abby asked, scrambling to catch up with her.

"I found a few friends to invite on our outing. I hope you don't mind." Wanda swept into the café and strode over to a table in the corner where Mary Pelsh sat with Emily Copeland and Clair Simmons. "Hello, ladies. Are you ready to go?"

Abby let out a delighted gasp. "Do not tell me you three are up for a little golf cart racing?"

"You know it," Clair said, grinning at Abby. "You girls have been going on and on about how much fun you have with these carts, so when Wanda invited us, we just had to say yes."

"Oh, Dad is going to be upset he missed out." Abby reached over and gave her father's long-term girlfriend a hug. "It's good to see you Clair. I'm sorry it's been so long."

"You've been busy running that potions business of yours and growing a little one. Don't think another thing of it." She got to her feet, and her companions followed. "All will be forgiven if you give me a rundown on the special features in your cart. The other ladies here nominated me to be the driver of our crew."

"Oh, I see. You three think you're racing me and Wanda?"

"Yep," Emily and Mary said at the same time.

"Don't forget about me," Hanna called, hurrying over to the group. "You're not leaving me out of the shenanigans."

Abby hugged her friend and said, "Never."

Wanda moved to Emily's side as the group made their way back out onto the sidewalk. "How are you and Dayton doing in the house? Are you settling in okay? Is there anything I need to make the owner aware of?"

Emily slipped her arm through Wanda's and beamed. "Not a thing, dear. The house is perfect. The town is perfect. My grandson is perfect. Now the only thing that would make me happier is if my son would get his head out of his backside and make up with the girl of his dreams." She grasped Wanda's arm and squeezed gently. "Don't let him push you away, Wanda. The Copeland men are passionate, and that sometimes means they overreact to things."

Unease settled in her stomach. "Did he, ah, tell you about our disagreement?"

"No, not the details anyway."

Thank the gods for that, Wanda thought.

"But he was upset when I saw him an hour ago. When I asked what happened, he just brushed me off and said you two had a disagreement and that he didn't want to talk about it. I just know him well enough to know that he holds things in until he explodes, and by then he's too far gone to have a constructive conversation. Whatever it is, I'm sure you two will work it out in time."

"I hope so," Wanda said, but she wasn't so sure. How could they fix what was wrong between them if they weren't on the same page?

"What's this? Trouble in paradise?" Abby asked Wanda. "Did you and Cameron have a fight?"

"Something like that," Wanda said dismissively. "But we're not here for a counseling session. We're here to kick some golf cart racing butt. Right?"

"Right!" Hanna cried out from right behind her. "Mom's going down," she added as she pointed at her mother, Mary.

Mary raised one eyebrow and smirked at her daughter. "We'll just see about that."

Wanda chuckled. She loved this new dynamic. Usually she raced her cart against Abby with each of them picking crew members from their core friend group. Then other times it was the women against the men. Honestly, those races were usually the most fun because the men mostly didn't know what they were doing when it came to the magic portion of the races. But she was willing to bet the trio from the café had some serious tricks up their sleeves.

"Looks like it's us three against the newcomers," Abby said, jumping into the driver's seat of her golf cart. "Let me just give Clair a lesson and then let's ride."

Wanda and Hanna retreated to Wanda's cart. Wanda waved a hand, dismissing the magical campfire, and then she turned on the party lights and cued up the radio. "Who do we want to listen to tonight?" she asked Hanna.

"Bruno Mars," her friend said without hesitation.

"Perfect." Wanda fiddled with the playlist and then sat back and waited for Abby.

It wasn't long before Abby was hurrying back over to Wanda's cart. She eyed Wanda in the driver's seat. "I think I should drive. I've beat you the last two times in our head-to-head races. You don't want to be known as the witch who lost to three novices do you?"

"Sit your tush down, Abigail Townsend. I could've won if I wanted to. I was just being nice to the pregnant lady."

Hanna snickered from the back seat.

"That's a lie and we both know it." Abby narrowed her eyes at Wanda but slipped into the passenger seat anyway. "You never let anyone win."

Wanda laughed because it was true. She loved competition and would never dream of losing anything on purpose. Still, she wasn't going to confirm anything for Abby. She knew her friend. Even though she said she didn't believe Wanda, there'd still be a bit of doubt. It was better to keep her guessing.

"Ready?" Wanda called over to Clair.

"Yeah, just give me a second and—" Clair pressed her foot to the pedal, and the golf cart shot out of the space and down Main Street toward the river with Clair handling it like she drove one every day of the week. The three older women howled with laughter while waving at Wanda, Abby, and Hanna.

"Oh, no she didn't," Wanda said with a laugh and took off after her.

"I thought you said she needed a lesson," Hanna asked Abby.

Abby shook her head and chuckled. "She obviously played me. She'll pay for that."

Wanda put the pedal to the floor, maxing out the speed, and then she hit the turbo button. The cart shot forward, sending them flying past their competition. Hanna turned around and made an obscene gesture, prompting her mother Mary to threaten to ground her.

Hanna snickered. "Sure, Mom. What are you gonna do? Get Rhys to lock me in my room?"

"She might like that!" Wanda called. Rhys was Hanna's

husband, and there was no doubt in Wanda's mind that he wouldn't mind having her all to himself for a week or two.

Mary Pelsh groaned and then laughed as she shook her head.

Wanda steered her cart onto the path that led to the river. Once she spotted the moonlight shining off the surface, she pulled to a stop and waited for the other cart to catch up.

"You kind of blew their doors off," Hanna said.

"Don't get too excited," Abby warned. "My cart goes a lot faster than that. Once they find the booster, they'll be fierce competition."

"And thank goodness for that," Wanda said. "It's no fun if the winning is easy."

Clair pulled Abby's cart to a stop right beside Wanda's. "There's nothing easy about the broads in this rig."

Wanda snorted. "No doubt. Now, do you know the rules?"

"There are no rules," Clair said.

"You got it!" Wanda said. "We go to where the tree line stops down there and turn around and come back. Whoever gets here first, wins."

"Perfect. Let's roll," Clair said, and her companions nodded.

Abby laughed and shook her head. "Okay, seriously, our official stance is that we don't have rules, but we are careful to be safe. Don't do anything that is going to send a cart into the river, blow up an engine, or otherwise cause an injury. Got it?"

"Yes, Mom," Clair, Mary, and Emily said in unison, sending Hanna and Wanda into a fit of laughter.

"Ha, ha," Abby said dryly. "You'll all thank me when everyone walks away from this with all of their limbs.

"We already do, Abs." Wanda winked at her. She glanced over at Clair. "This time we'll start when Emily yells go. Okay, Emily?"

"Perfect." Emily Copeland sat in the back of Abby's cart with a huge smile on her face. Wanda felt her heart swell with joy just looking at the woman. That's how Wanda always saw herself, and she made a vow to stop focusing on the drama in her life and just enjoy each moment as it came.

"Ready? Set! Go!" Emily cried.

Clair shot forward, while Wanda, who'd been too busy contemplating her own state of mind, hadn't been ready.

"Oh, crap!" Wanda cried and sent the cart flying forward. "Sorry, ladies. My bad."

But neither Abby nor Hanna answered. They were too busy already casting spells left and right, trying to slow down the other cart.

Abby, who was an earth witch, was busy adding dirt speed bumps in front of her cart, while Hanna, a water witch, was using the water from the river to make it storm. The combined effect had already turned their path into a mud pit, slowing them down enough that Wanda shot right past them.

"Nice work, girls," Wanda said with a laugh. "That trick never fails." Their cart sailed to the turnaround point with ease, and Wanda thought they'd win this race without too much difficulty. But just as soon as the thought popped into her head, a mass of something reddish brown started to move toward them from the trees.

"What the heck is that?" Abby asked, squinting at the blob.

"Looks like a giant pile of pine needles," Hanna said.

"That's not going to be fun if they hit us with that,' Wanda said as she steered the cart closer to the river, trying to get out of the blob's path. But it was no use; the blob seemed to be on a direct path with their cart.

"What do they have? A homing device to track us?" Hanna asked.

"I bet it's your mother doing this," Abby said. "That woman is wicked with her air magic."

"Isn't Clair an air witch, too?" Hanna asked.

"No, she's an earth witch, but I've never seen her use her magic much," Abby said.

"If they're combining that magic, we're never going to outrun it. Time to play some chicken." Wanda steered the cart straight for the blob, intending to dart either right or left when it was about to hit them. But before they got to it, the blob morphed and turned into the image of a man. A naked man made of pine needles.

"What the hell?" Hanna cried. "Did my mother put a penis on her pine needle Bigfoot?"

Abby cackled. "She sure did. And, oh my goddess above. Piney is doing a dance for us."

"He's swinging his junk and flexing as if he were a Thunder from Down Under dancer. In fact... oh, no. My mother has been to a Thunder from Down Under show?"

Wanda was laughing so hard that tears were streaming down her face and she was having trouble breathing. The pine needle Bigfoot was hilarious, but Hanna's reaction was the icing on the cake.

"Enjoy, ladies! Make sure to put a tip in his G-string," Mary called as the other cart flew by them.

"Wanda!" Hanna snapped. "Go! They're going to win!"

Hanna's cry snapped Wanda out of her hysterics. Then with a flick of her wrist, she sent a ball of fire in Piney's direction. The moment it hit him the formation scattered, and the fire was out even before the debris hit the ground.

"Go! Go! Go!" Abby cried.

Wanda pressed her foot down on the pedal, but as soon as she did, she saw movement a few feet in front of the cart and slammed on the brakes. The cart jerked to a stop.

"What are you doing?" Abby shouted. "They're going to win!"

"There's something moving in front of the cart." She hopped out and hurried to where she saw the movement. Whatever it was, it was covered in the mud Abby and Hanna had created, and Wanda just hoped it wasn't a skunk or a rat or something else equally as horrifying. It didn't take long for her to notice the big brown eyes and bright pink tongue.

"Oh my goodness," Abby said. "That's a puppy."

Wanda crouched down and put her hand out to the creature, who her hand and then licked her fingers. "Hey, puppers. You lost?"

The puppy scrambled through the mud and immediately curled up at her feet, shaking from the cold. "It's okay, little one. We've got you." She glanced up and spotted Hanna standing next to the cart. "Hanna, I have a sweatshirt under the back seat. Can you get it for me?"

"Sure." A moment later, Hanna handed her the gray sweatshirt.

Wanda quickly wrapped the puppy up and then retreated to the passenger seat. "Abs? Can you drive?"

"Sure." Abby and Hanna jumped back into the cart and the three of them went to meet the current champions of the ongoing golf cart races.

CHAPTER 18

It had been four days since Cameron had stormed out of Wanda's house, and they hadn't spoken since. And it was killing him. He recognized that he hadn't exactly handled the situation very well. But damn, he'd been hurt when she implied they weren't serious. He'd just opened up to her, shared a lot of very personal stuff with her, and then when they'd made love, he'd never felt closer to anyone. He just didn't understand how she hadn't felt it too.

Was he crazy? Was it possible that everything was one-sided and she didn't feel what he did? It had happened with Tori. He'd been convinced that they were in love. That she was happy in their relationship and everything was great. But then she left, and it was clear he'd misread the entire situation. There was no reason to believe it wasn't the same with Wanda. Maybe he was just bad at this.

It was why he hadn't called. He didn't trust himself to read their situation clearly. If she wanted something with him, she was going to need to make the first move. He didn't want to push her into anything. If she felt something for him, she'd call, right?

Cameron jammed his hands into his jean pockets and walked into the Townsend brewpub. He was meeting his mother for burgers while his father was busy talking about orchards with Lincoln Townsend. His parents had progressed from just getting a house in Keating Hollow to considering a small farm.

Once they'd come up with that idea, his father made appointments to talk to Lincoln Townsend about his apple orchard and the Pelshes about their winery. He wanted to know the economics of farming in Keating Hollow before they made any other plans. Dayton Copeland had grown up on a farm, so he knew about growing things. Cameron just never thought his parents might end up owning one in their retirement years. It would be a lot of work, but his parents had the resources to hire help. If it was what they wanted, he'd support them one hundred percent.

Cameron moved through the pub toward the bar, but before he reached his destination, a familiar voice called, "Hey, Dad!"

He froze, pleasantly surprised to hear Cam call him dad as if he'd been calling him that all of his life. Cameron turned and spotted his son sitting with his boss, Hunter McCormick. Both of them were wearing work-worn jeans and T-shirts, and despite looking exhausted from a long day of labor, they were smiling as if they had something to celebrate.

Cam waved him over and pointed to the empty chair next to him.

"Hello," Cameron said as he took a seat. "You two look happy. Good day at work?"

"Hey, Cameron," Hunter said. "You should be very proud of your boy here. He caught a mistake in the measurements for the kitchen on our current job that would've cost us thousands. The kid is amazing. I've never had someone working for me that has his level of attention to detail. I'm so impressed that I've waived the ninety-day probation period and not only made him a permanent hire but gave him a raise, too. Can't let good talent get away."

"Wow. Impressive." Cameron clapped his son on the back. "Well done, Cam."

His son flushed and looked both pleased and a little bit embarrassed at the praise.

"Can't tell you how happy I am to have him on staff," Hunter continued. "He's reliable, always on time, and he's making himself indispensable. I wish I had ten more just like him."

Cameron wasn't sure if it was even his place to feel pride, but he did, even though he hadn't had any hand in raising him or instilling that kind of work ethic. He was so damned proud to call him his son that he was nearly bursting with it. He smiled at Cam and then turned to Hunter. "That's definitely great to hear."

"Well, I've got to get going. Faith is waiting for me." Hunter threw a couple of bills on the table, presumably to cover the drinks they'd had, and then clasped Cam on the shoulder. "Great work today, kid. See you in the morning."

"I'll be there," Cam said. "Thanks for the soda, and well… everything."

"No thanks necessary. You earned it." Hunter nodded to Cameron before heading out of the pub.

"Have you eaten yet?" Cameron asked his son.

Cam shook his head.

"Then how about I buy you a celebration dinner?" When Cam grinned and nodded, Cameron waved Sadie over. She took their order for burgers, wings, and nachos. Cameron ordered a beer, while Cam opted for iced tea.

"I'll have these right up." Sadie hurried off to her next table.

"So, looks like your stay here in Keating Hollow is permanent," Cameron said.

Cam nodded. "What about you? Any plans of relocating?"

Cameron pursed his lips. "I'm thinking about it. There are a couple of really good reasons to stay. Your grandparents are getting more and more serious about making the move permanent, and you're here."

"Not to mention Wanda," Cam said with a knowing smile.

Cameron sidestepped the topic of Wanda. There was no question that she was part of the equation that made him consider Keating Hollow. She was a big part of it, actually, but considering the way they'd left things a few days ago, he was trying to not factor her into his decision. There was no guarantee that they'd work out. "Miranda is here, too. If *Fire Valley* takes off, it's going to be a lot easier to work on upcoming seasons if we're both living in the same place."

"Sounds like there's not much to think about." Cam took a drink of his water while he watched his father.

Cameron chuckled. "You know what? You're right. There really isn't. But there are some logistics to work out. I still have a house in Hollywood that I'll need to deal with. Shouldn't be too much of a hassle, though."

Cam sat back in his chair, looking relaxed and at home in the pub. It certainly seemed that Keating Hollow agreed with him.

"You seem… settled. That's different from when we first

met. I think Keating Hollow agrees with you," Cameron observed.

"You could say that. I've got a decent apartment, a great job with a great boss, family I didn't know existed a few months ago, and Blake. It's more than I hoped for, honestly."

Cameron clasped his son's shoulder and squeezed. "I'm really happy for you, son. And just in case you didn't know it, I'm really glad you sought me out. I couldn't be happier to be your father."

"Me too. Honestly, meeting you and my grandparents is what gave me the courage to look for Jessie."

"Did you find her?" Cameron asked, not exactly sure how he felt about that. A small part of him was jealous that this woman got to be a part of Cam's childhood when he hadn't. But there was a larger part of him that hoped Cam got the answers he deserved.

"I did." He pressed his lips together, looking nervous. "She really wants to see me and suggested that she and her partner come here for Valentine's weekend. She said they'd been planning a trip to the coast anyway. They'd just modify it to come here." He took another long sip of his water then said, "I told her yes. I hope that wasn't a mistake."

Cameron squeezed his shoulder again. "I'm sure no matter what, it will be the closure you need. And if it's rough, your grandparents and I will still be here."

Relief washed over Cam's features as he gave his father a grateful smile. "Thanks for that."

"And hey, it doesn't hurt to remember that you're doing great. Nothing Jessie could say will change that. Like you said, you've got a great job, a nice place to live, me and your grandparents, and Blake." Cameron winked at him. "Everything else is just icing."

"Would you... um, consider coming along when I talk to her?" Cam asked.

Cameron raised both eyebrows in surprise. He hadn't been expecting that. He'd love to ask Jessie some questions if she was willing to answer them, but he in no way wanted to be a distraction for their reunion. "You want me there?"

Cam nodded.

"I will if you want me to, but I certainly don't want to intrude."

"You're not intruding," Cam said earnestly. "I think we both deserve answers, and after talking to her, it sounds like Jessie might have them."

"Then just let me know when and where, and I'll be there."

"My boys!" Cameron's mother's voice echoed through the brewpub. "I'm so glad you're both here," she said when she reached their table. "I wasn't expecting you, Cam, so this is a great surprise."

"Hi, Mom." Cameron rose and gave his mother a kiss on the cheek. "We already ordered. I got you that burger you raved about, but if you want something else, I'm sure Sadie can rustle up a menu for you."

"Oh, no. A burger is fine. And I'm starving, so this is perfect." She leaned over and gave Cam a hug. "You're looking good, Cam. Did you have a good day?"

Cam shared his good news and beamed when she told him how proud she was of him.

"It's no surprise you're such a dedicated worker." Emily said. "Cameron and his father have both always had an excellent work ethic. Just following in the family footsteps."

"It's good to know it's in my genes," Cam said with a laugh. "Now tell me about you. What have you been up to?"

"So much. You have no idea. I love it here. Just the other night, I had a girls' night with Mary Pelsh and Clair Simmons. Mary owns Incantation Café, and Clair is Lincoln Townsend's significant other. Anyway, we got together for coffee and ended up racing golf carts with Wanda, Hanna, and Abby. No one expected us to win, but we put on one heck of a magic show for those ladies, and they ended up eating our dust. It was so much fun. I can't wait to do it again."

Cameron's ears picked up when his mother mentioned Wanda. He wanted to ask how she was, if she seemed happy, or tired, or sad. It seemed unreal that she'd lost the golf cart race to three older ladies. Not that his mother wasn't capable. She was. But golf cart racing was sort of a religion for Wanda and Abby. He was dying to know what happened. But instead of asking questions, he said nothing and listened to his son and his mother chatter on about everything they loved about Keating Hollow.

In that moment, he realized that he was indeed going to make the town his home. Even though he'd told Cam earlier that there really wasn't much to think about when deciding to move to town, he hadn't really made the decision. He'd still been wondering if it was the right move. Now, he could see there really was no question about it.

CHAPTER 19

Wanda held the phone to her ear and watched as the fluffy golden puppy rolled around on her kitchen floor. After she'd rescued the little one from the mud, she'd taken her home, cleaned her up, fed her some rice and chicken, and then taken her to the healer first thing the next morning. After she'd been treated for a mild case of dehydration with some healing potions, she'd been given a clean bill of health.

"Is there any word on who this puppy might belong to?" Wanda asked the healer. They'd taken a description of the puppy and promised to check around to see if she had a family already.

"I'm sorry, Wanda. Nothing," the healer said. "We've checked with our contacts at all the local shelters and sent an email out to the surrounding pet healer offices, but so far no one is claiming that sweet girl. At this point, you might want to decide what it is you want. Are you interested in adopting her, or do you want us to find her a home? She's so cute and sweet, I'm sure it won't take any time at all."

Wanda crouched down and petted the puppy's sweet round belly. Immediately the pup rolled over and tried to jump into her arms. They'd been together for a little over a week, and in that time the puppy had followed Wanda everywhere and even staked out a spot on Wanda's bed at night. The pup nudged Wanda's hand, indicating she wanted more pets. As Wanda scratched behind her ear, the little one looked up at her with the most loving brown eyes Wanda had ever seen. There was no question about it. "I'll adopt her."

The healer chuckled. "I'm not surprised. All right then, let's set up her next puppy wellness check in a couple of weeks. Maybe by then you'll have a name picked out."

"We're working on it." After Wanda ended the call, she scooped the puppy up and cradled her against her chest. "What do you think? Princess Penelope? Lady Louise? Countess Camila?"

"She's a goldendoodle, not royalty," Blake said as she entered the kitchen.

"Tell her that." Wanda touched her nose to the pup's and said, "You can be a princess if you want to be."

"Whatever." Blake opened the refrigerator and pulled out a stick of string cheese. "Doesn't matter to me. I'll still call her Chewbarka. That little terror ruined my phone charger and ate my toothbrush."

"She's still a puppy. She just doesn't know any better yet. We need to do a better job of puppy proofing the house." Wanda studied her. "Are you okay? You don't really seem yourself. Did something happen at school today?"

"Nope. Just tired. Chewbarka kept me up last night with her whining."

Wanda opened her mouth to protest her claim, but before

she could get the words out, Blake was gone again. She turned her attention to the puppy and sighed. "That was rude, don't you think?"

The puppy blinked at her.

"I know. You had a major milestone last night. You didn't wake up once, and I'd know because I'm the one who takes you out." She patted her pup's head and said, "Don't worry. She'll come around."

The puppy snuggled into Wanda's chest, making Wanda melt into a puddle of goo. Who knew having a puppy would turn her into the world's biggest sap? It didn't matter. She loved her sweet little fluff ball, and that was all there was to it.

"So, names. We're not using Chewbarka. That's just setting expectations too low, and we're going to get past this phase. Don't you worry. How about Noodle? Or Sprout? Or something cooler like Nyx or Calypso? Oh, I know! Lyric. That's perfect. We'll tell Blake we used Chewbarka as inspiration. Get it? Bark and Lyric? Oh never mind. Lyric it is."

With the puppy still in her arms, Wanda climbed the stairs to share her decision with Blake. She found her sister lying on her bed, frowning at her phone.

"Hey," Wanda said. "I came to let you know we settled on Lyric."

"What?" Blake didn't even turn to look at her.

"I've decided to name the puppy Lyric."

Blake finally cut her gaze to Wanda and the puppy. "That's actually kinda cute. I'm still going to call her—"

"Chewbarka, we know. That's fine. She'll win you over eventually."

"You think?" Blake studied the puppy, who was curled up

against Wanda looking cuter than ever. "Maybe. She's sweet when she's sleeping."

Wanda shook her head and almost made a joke about her being damaged, because who didn't love adorable little puppies, but she held back at the last second. Her sister had been hot and cold for days now, and Wanda strongly suspected she was having a hard time adjusting to her new life in Keating Hollow. The only time she seemed to be genuinely happy was when she was talking to Cam or headed out to see him.

She wanted to suggest that Blake see a professional to do a mental health check-in, but the one time she'd brought it up, Blake had firmly told her she wasn't interested and then clammed up for the next twenty-four hours.

Wanda sucked in a breath and braced herself for any sort of response. "Blake, I know you said you're just tired, but are you sure you're okay? You seem… not really yourself."

Blake let out an exaggerated sigh, the kind that teenagers were famous for, and said, "I'm *fine.* What else do you want from me?"

Now that just pissed Wanda off. Still, she controlled herself, and in what she hoped was a nonconfrontational tone, she said, "Well, I'd love to know how you're doing at school without having to check the computer for your grades. And how work is going, if you like it or if you're thinking you might try somewhere else during the tourist season."

Wanda clutched Lyric closer to her body, and even though she desperately just wanted to do whatever she wanted when it came to the puppy, she really needed Blakes input. This was her home too. "Then I'd like to know how you really feel about the puppy. I've completely fallen for her, but if you have strong feelings either way, I'd like to weigh them in on my decision to keep her. I already told the healer that we'd adopt her, but if that's not a good idea, I'm sure we can find someone who would be thrilled to have her."

Blake put her phone down and stared at her sister for minute, her expression unreadable. Then she cleared her throat and said, "School is going all right. I got a B on my English test, an A on my math test, and turned in a week's worth of chemistry homework after getting Cam's help. Work is fine. Candy and I are thinking of doing something this weekend. And you should keep the puppy. It's obvious you love her."

"Okay. Well, that all sounds good," Wanda said, wondering if she'd been the problem all along. Had she not been asking the right questions? Because that was the most direct answer she'd gotten all week.

Blake turned back to her phone, obviously dismissing Wanda.

Wanda wanted to scream. Had she been like that as a teenager? Uncommunicative and distant? She supposed she was sometimes, but probably not much. Wanda was far too outgoing and always had to tell her mother about everything going on in her life.

The thought of her mom triggered a bone-deep sadness. Damn, she missed her. It had just been Wanda and her mom after her dad left. They'd been closer than mother and daughter probably should've been. And it was times like this, when she had a hard time communicating with Blake, that she missed her mom most. What she would've given to be able to ask for her advice about Blake or Cameron. Or just hug her and know she wasn't alone in this world.

"Stop it, Wanda. You aren't alone," she muttered to

herself. "You have plenty of family. Stop feeling sorry for yourself."

She heard Blake's phone ring and Blake answer it a second later.

"Hi, Cam." Her voice was soft and sweet, and just like always, she sounded happy.

At least one of us has a successful love life, Wanda thought and headed back downstairs.

Wanda went into the kitchen, made herself a sandwich for dinner, and then curled up on the couch with the puppy. It wasn't long before she heard Blake's footsteps on the stairs. Wanda placed her empty plate on the side table and called, "There's leftovers in the fridge if you're hungry. Or stuff for sandwiches."

"I'm really not that hungry," Blake said, stopping at the bottom of the stairs.

"Okay. It's there if you get hungry later."

"Um, actually, I was coming down to tell you that Candy invited me out to the beach tonight." Blake fidgeted with the hem of her shirt as she continued. "It's for a couple of nights actually. I guess there are cabins at the beach, and she and another friend reserved one. They invited me along. Are you okay with that?"

"It's kind of last minute don't you think?" Wanda said and immediately grimaced. "Good goddess, I sound like a paranoid parent who doesn't trust their kid. Sorry. That just took me off guard. When you said earlier that you might be going out with Candy, I didn't figure it would be a weekend getaway."

Blake chuckled and shook her head. "I wouldn't know anything about that. The parentals never cared what I did. Most of the time I didn't even tell them."

Suddenly her sister's behavior made a lot more sense. Wanda suspected that she wasn't intentionally keeping things from her. She just wasn't used to answering to anyone. "That's just sad, Blake. I knew they weren't model parents, but I'm sorry they didn't even seem to care."

She shrugged. "Grandma did. At least she cared... and now you."

Wanda grinned at her, feeling as if they might've just had some sort of breakthrough. The beach cabins weren't that far away. Wanda even knew exactly where they were. This time of year, they wouldn't be busy, so she didn't worry too much about teenage girls getting into trouble. "Go ahead with Candy and her friend. I'm sure you'll have a great time. Just be careful and don't let anyone talk you into something you don't want to do."

Blake nodded. "I've got it covered."

"I'm sure you do." She pursed her lips and remembered how Candy had nearly totaled her aunt's car the first time she drove it. "You know what? Why don't you take my car? I know the one Candy's driving these days isn't the most reliable. That way I'll worry less."

"Are you sure?" Blake asked. "How will you get around?"

"I've got my handy golf cart. I use it more often anyway."

"That's generous. Thank you." She started back up the stairs, but after a few steps she paused and glanced over her shoulder. "Really, thanks, Wanda."

"For what?"

"Being you."

CHAPTER 20

After Blake left for the weekend, Wanda took the puppy out and then went back inside, prepared to curl up for the rest of the night with Netflix and a pint of ice cream. She deserved it. Right? Her sister was off having fun with new friends while she sat at home wondering if she was ever going to hear from Cameron again.

It had been over a week since they'd spoken. She'd thought about calling, but he'd been so upset, she thought maybe she should wait for him to make the first move. She didn't want to give the impression that she'd changed her mind. In fact, after her little breakthrough with Blake, she was more convinced than ever she was making the right decision. If she was busy running around with Cameron, she might not be there when Blake needed her most.

She sighed and took a bite of the chocolate caramel swirl she saved for the nights when she was really feeling sorry for herself.

Wanda picked up the remote and turned the television on, hoping she'd find something worth watching that she hadn't seen already. But before she started browsing, her phone started playing "You've Got a Friend," indicating that Abby was calling. Wanda silently patted herself on the back for that one. It was exactly what she needed to hear.

"Hi, Abs. What's up?"

"Olive is at her grandmother's, and Clay is working. He and Rhys have been tweaking the specialty summer brews and I'm a work widow… again." Clay was the manager at the Townsend brewpub and a talented brewmaster. He was always busy this time of year while they worked hard to stock up for the summer season.

"Okay. How can I help with that? Do you want to come over? I have ice cream and Netflix."

Abby chuckled. "I'm not so far gone that I'm already spending my Friday nights eating a pint of ice cream. That activity is reserved for emergencies only. You know that."

Wanda glanced around at her pint of ice cream, the remote on the table, and her outfit of yoga pants and a T-shirt that was so old the silkscreened image of Prince had all but faded away. All on a Friday night before seven o'clock. If this was what her life was like before she even turned thirty-five, what was forty going to look like? "What did you have in mind?"

"Hanna and I are going over to her parents' winery to check out their newest offerings. You interested?"

"Can I bring Lyric?" she asked, not sure she should leave the puppy home alone. She had a crate, but so far she hadn't used it much.

"Who's Lyric?" Abby asked.

"The puppy. If I don't bring her, she'll be home all alone."

"Where's Blake?"

"Out with friends," Wanda said, already moving toward the kitchen to put the ice cream back in the freezer.

"I'm sure it's fine. Mary will probably lose her mind once she sees that little fluff ball of sweetness again," Abby said. "You want me to come get you, or do you want to pick me up? I'm at my dad's right now. His anniversary with Clair is tomorrow, and Dad wants to surprise her with a romantic homemade dinner. He has the dinner covered but asked if I'd make some chocolate covered strawberries for dessert. I, of course, added a little something extra to spice things up a bit. Now I need to get out of here before I start thinking about what that actually means."

Wanda cackled. Abby was an earth witch who specialized in energy potions and high-end skin products. When she said she'd spiced up the chocolate, what she meant was she'd added something to turn those strawberries into an aphrodisiac. "You mean you're playing sex therapist for your dad and Clair?"

"No!" she insisted. "Just doing what I'd do for any of my friends who were celebrating a romantic milestone."

"Sure, Abs. Whatever you say. That means you're on the way to the Pelshes. I should come to you, but Blake has my car, so that means we'll be riding in the golf cart."

"Not a problem. It's not that cold out. See you soon." Abby ended the call.

Wanda tossed her phone onto the coffee table and bounded up the stairs with the puppy right behind her. She needed to lose the yoga pants and find a shirt that didn't have holes in the pits.

~

"Oh. Em. Gee," Abby exclaimed when she jumped into Wanda's golf cart and pulled the puppy into her lap. "Lyric is the cutest freakin' thing I've ever seen."

"She's a heartbreaker for sure." Wanda took off down the long driveway of the Townsend compound. The tree-lined mile-long drive was lit up with tiny white twinkle lights, making the property appear magical. She loved the Townsend property and often thought that she'd love to buy some acreage nearby and start her own compound. But she just didn't know if she was up to maintaining that much land all on her own. She knew it was a good investment, she just didn't know if it was the right move for her.

"So," Abby said. "What's going on with you and Cameron?"

Wanda groaned. "New subject please."

"Really, Wanda?" Abby shook her head. "You're not going to tell me, your oldest friend who already knows the rest of your secrets?"

"I don't have any new secrets," Wanda insisted. "It's been over a week since we talked. I'm not sure we're compatible."

"*Compatible*? You've got to be kidding me." Abby stared at her with an incredulous look on her face. "I have never seen two people more perfect for each other. What is it, babe? What's going on?"

"We're not perfect for each other. He wants… well, promises and forever. I can't do that. Nor did I ever pretend I could. If I didn't have Blake here, then maybe things could be different, but even then, forever? You know I'm not the forever kind of girl."

Abby stroked the puppy's head while she took in that information. Then she sighed. "That sounds like a real problem. But let me ask you one thing."

"What's that?" Wanda asked.

"Are you certain you don't want any part of forever? No long-term relationship where you can share your life with someone else? Someone you love and trust and will help you share the burdens and joys of this life we're all living?"

"Damn, Abs. Why'd you have to put that out there?" Wanda asked, grimacing.

Abby chuckled. "Because I'm your best friend and I will always ask the hard questions and push you when I think you need to be pushed. Now, are you sure you want to be perpetually single if it means letting someone go who is important to you?"

Wanda cut her gaze to her friend and narrowed her eyes. "Are you saying there's something wrong with not wanting to be a part of a 'forever' with someone? That singlehood is less than?"

"What?" Abby cried, looking taken aback as she scowled at Wanda. "Of course not. You know me better than that. When have I ever asked you if you were sure you wanted to dump someone or questioned why you've been single for the past how many years?"

"Never." It was true. Abby hadn't ever asked why Wanda didn't have a significant other, or if she wanted to get married, or even if her biological clock was ticking. There were plenty of other people in Keating Hollow who had that line of questioning covered. But never Abby.

"Okay, then I think it's obvious that I'm only asking because what you have with Cameron is clearly different than the rest of them, and I don't want you to regret letting him go a year or two from now because you were too scared to take a chance."

"I'm not scared," Wanda said automatically.

Abby gave Wanda the side-eye and snorted her disagreement. "Uh-huh."

Crap. It didn't pay to lie to her best friend. "Okay, fine. I'm terrified. But not for the reason you think."

"What do I think?" Abby asked, sounding curious now.

"I'm not afraid of Cameron leaving. I'm afraid that *I* will. I'm always the one who walks away. I can't do that to him. Not again."

"When did you walk away before?"

"Not me. His college girlfriend. Cam's mom. Cameron was going to ask her to marry him, but before he had a chance, she just left with no explanation. I don't think he ever fully recovered, and I don't want to be the person who puts him through that again. Plus, I'm worried about Blake. If I start a relationship with him and it doesn't work out, how will she feel? She's been through so much already, and I don't want to risk adding to that pain."

Abby shook her head. "First, you're not a nineteen-year-old college student. So thinking you'll do anything remotely close to what Cam's mom did seems pretty far-fetched. But I get your meaning. You're scared you'll hurt him."

"Yeah."

"But you already did that by pushing him away, Wanda. Can't you see that?" Abby reached over and squeezed her hand as she added, "And as far as what this might do to Blake, well, I think that's a bunch of crap. I don't think I need to explain why. Just trust yourself, babe. You're a great friend with the biggest heart I've ever known. You're not just going to throw away the man you choose to share your life with. That's not who you are."

Hadn't she already though? She'd let him walk out of her

house and then not bothered to call and try to clear the air. "It might be too late anyway."

"Oh, I doubt it. Just call him when you get home. I bet you two will patch this up fairly quickly once you talk it out."

"Maybe." Wanda pulled the golf cart into a parking space on the Pelshes' property and turned the cart off. "Right now, I really need a glass or three of wine." It was then she glanced at her friend and the barely there baby bump and said, "Sampling wines, Abs? Really?"

Abby rolled her eyes. "I'm not sampling them. I'll be sampling the pies Mary's been making to sell as an add-on."

"Glad to hear it. Now lead on. Pie sounds fantastic."

CHAPTER 21

Wanda held Lyric in her arms as she followed Abby into the Pelshes' brand-new tasting room. It was a large space with tables set up on one side, presumably for the pie-eating section, and a bar on the other with a generous amount of seating for wine tasting. One of the tables was occupied by Lincoln Townsend and Walter Pelsh.

As Abby and Wanda approached to say their hellos, Wanda overheard them talking about the ten acres that separated their two properties.

"I think Dayton Copeland is going to be a fine neighbor," Lin said. "I can't imagine starting a farm from scratch at our age, but he seems serious about it. Said he'd always wanted to get back to farming, so now that he had the opportunity, he was going for it."

"Did he say what he wanted to farm?" Walter asked and then took a sip of what appeared to be whiskey. She would've laughed, considering they were at a winery, but she was too busy trying to make sense of what they were talking about.

"He's open to apples, pears, grapes, or cherries, but I'm trying to steer him into apples. It'll take a few years to produce a decent yield, but with the way our cider business is taking off, we are likely going to need to start purchasing apples instead of relying only on my farm. We just can't keep up. I'd love to buy from my neighbor."

"Blueberries would be good, too," Walter added. "I hear there's a decent market for blueberry wine. I'd like to try it, but my land is full of grapes."

"I'm sure he'd be open to it. Let him know the next time you talk to him."

Abby cleared her throat. "Excuse me gentlemen. Wanda and I don't want to interrupt, but we did want to say hi." She leaned over and gave her dad a kiss. "Always talking business, aren't you?"

He smiled up at her. "It's in my blood, baby girl."

"Don't I know it. The strawberries are in the fridge, by the way. I'm sure Clair will love them.

"Thanks, sweetheart. I owe you one. Are you two here for Mary's pie?"

"We sure are," Wanda said and kissed his other cheek. "Good to see you, Lincoln."

"You, too. And who's this gorgeous girl?" he asked while petting the puppy's head.

"Lyric. She was lost and alone down by the river. I took her in to help her out, but now I'm smitten, so it looks like she's here to stay."

Abby turned her attention to Mr. Pelsh and gave him a big smile. "Hope we're not sneaking any of your personal stash."

"Girl, Mary has more pies than will fit in that subzero refrigerator I got for her. You eat as much pie as you can handle. I'll consider it a personal favor."

"Awesome. Not only do I not have to feel guilty, but I can pretend I'm doing this for a good cause."

Walter chuckled and turned to Wanda. "Hello, there, Wanda. Looks like you've got a loyal companion, there."

She glanced down at the snoozing dog in her arms and nodded. "Definitely. I haven't had any privacy since she moved in."

Walter laughed. "That's a dog for you. Best creatures on earth though."

Wanda had to agree, and she'd only been a dog mom for a week.

"How are you and your sister doing?" he asked.

"Good, thank you. She's actually with Candy this weekend over at the beach. I'm glad she's—"

"Candy's not at the beach," Walter said. "She's in the kitchen with Mary, helping her with the pies. And tomorrow she's headed up to Vancouver for the weekend to spend some time with Silas and Levi before they come home for that wedding on Valentine's Day."

"Shannon and Brian's wedding," Abby added helpfully.

"What do you mean Candy is here? Are you saying she was never going to the beach this weekend?"

"Not that I'm aware of, and since I bought her ticket to Canada, I'm pretty sure I got that right," he said.

"Uncle Walter," Candy called as she walked in carrying a tray of pies. She was in jeans, a Pelsh winery T-shirt, and a red apron that had flour smudges on it, indicating that she had indeed been helping Mary with the pies. "Did you want blackberry, cherry, or peach?"

"Peach. Like always," he said. "While you're here, have you talked to Wanda's sister today?"

"Nope. Not since yesterday, why?"

"Wanda, you're up," Mr. Pelsh said as he rose from his spot at the table to retrieve the pies from his niece. "I'll deal with these."

"More like eat a piece from all of them," Candy teased. Once her hands were free, she turned to Wanda. "Is something wrong? Is Blake okay?"

"That's the question, isn't it? She told me she was headed to the coast with you and another friend tonight to stay in one of the beach cabins over the weekend. Only she left a couple hours ago and you're here and apparently ready to go to Canada tomorrow."

Candy grimaced and shook her head. "I can't believe she used me as an excuse. Dang, a heads-up would've been nice."

Wanda narrowed her eyes at her.

"Sorry, ma'am. I… never mind. We did talk about renting one of those cabins in the spring when it's a little warmer, but no, we did not have plans this weekend. I'm sorry."

"Son of a… ugh." Wanda pulled out her phone and called her sister. The call went straight to voice mail. Of course it did. She did the same with Cam and was grateful she had his number from when she'd helped him find his place. His phone rang three times before voice mail picked up. "Cam, it's Wanda Danvers, and I could really use your help. Blake has taken off for the weekend, and it turns out she didn't go with the person she said she was going with, and now I'm worried. Please call me as soon as you get this. Thanks."

She tried her sister again and cursed when it went straight to voice mail.

Without overthinking it, she called Cameron. He

answered on the first ring. "Wanda, I'm so glad you called. I've been meaning to—"

"Cameron listen, I'm calling about Blake."

"Is she okay?" he asked, the concern in his tone unmistakable.

"I have no idea. She left tonight and claimed to be going to a cabin at the beach for the weekend with Candy. But as it turns out, Candy isn't with her and knew nothing about it. Now I'm freaking out, and the only other person I can imagine she'd be with is Cam, but he isn't answering either and now I don't know what to do."

"Where are you?" he asked.

"The Pelshes' winery."

"I'll be right there. We'll find Cam and look for her together. Okay?"

She nodded, even though she knew he couldn't see her, and then finally said, "Yes. I'll wait for you."

The call ended, and Wanda suddenly felt like the day had lasted forty-eight hours instead of twenty-four. She sank down into one of the chairs and tried her best not to panic.

"Wanda, is there anything I can do?" Abby asked, placing a hand on Lyric. "Want me to take her and your golf cart? That way you can just come to my house to pick them up when you're ready."

She glanced at her dog and then at her friend and found herself nodding. "Yes, please. She's still really needy, so beware."

"I've got this,' Abby said. "You forget we are a dog family. I know what to do." She pulled Lyric out of Wanda's hands and kissed the pup on top of her head. Lyric turned her head and returned the kiss with a lot of tongue. "That was more than I bargained for. It's a good thing you're cute, little one."

Lyric looked up at her with her gorgeous eyes and in that moment, Wanda knew Abby was a goner. The dog was a hypnotist at best. At worst, she was a master manipulator. Either way, Abby was watching the puppy, which meant Wanda was free to find her sister. As soon as she heard a vehicle outside, she darted out and ran straight into Cameron's arms.

CHAPTER 22

"It's okay." Cameron wrapped his arms around Wanda and felt the dull ache in his chest disappear. For the past week, he'd been walking around pretending to be whole, but he wasn't. He'd left a part of himself back at her house the day he stormed out of her bedroom, and he hadn't been right since. "We'll find her."

"But what if she lied to me about where she was going?" Wanda asked, looking up at him with fear in her eyes. It wasn't an emotion he'd ever seen in her expression, and it unsettled him. The Wanda he knew was fearless.

"Then we'll still find her somehow, or she'll call when she's ready. Just try to remember that she's been taking care of herself for a long time now. That seventeen-year-old got on a bus, traveled across the country, and ended up on your doorstep without your number or your address. She can take care of herself, right?"

Wanda pulled back and dabbed at her watery eyes. "Yeah. Okay. Good point."

"Come on." He tugged her toward his SUV. "Let's start at Cam's place. We'll see if he's home and just not answering."

Wanda doubted that very much. She was certain that the two were together, she just didn't know where or why Blake lied to her. Would Wanda have let Blake go if she knew her sister was planning an overnight with Cam?

No. She definitely wouldn't have been on board with that. Her sister was only seventeen, and the two teenagers had only known each other for a few weeks. She understood that Blake had been on her own for a long time, and that her parents hadn't cared enough to actually parent, but Wanda cared. She cared a lot, and no matter what Blake thought, she needed boundaries and rules. She needed to know someone was looking out for her.

"I don't think I'm cut out to be a parent," Wanda said as Cameron steered the SUV down the Pelshes' long driveway.

"What? You already are a parent, and as near as I can tell, a pretty fantastic one," Cameron said.

"That's not how I feel, but thanks for saying that," she said.

He reached over and took her hand with his and was gratified when she didn't pull away.

"Do you think they're together?" Wanda asked.

"Most likely. If we can find Cam, we'll find her. The good thing is that if they are together, then Cam will take care of her," he said, hoping that statement was true. Cameron couldn't imagine why Cam would take off with Blake without making sure Wanda knew where they were or what they were up to. It seemed so out of character for the young man he was getting to know.

Wanda sucked in a deep breath and let it out but didn't respond.

He suspected that anything else he said at that point wouldn't do any good anyway, so he stayed quiet until he rounded the corner of Gideon's gravel driveway and spotted Wanda's red Honda CRV parked in front of the garage.

"I guess that answers the question as to whether or not she's with Cam," Cameron said, parking next to the CRV.

Wanda hopped out and hurried up the stairs to Cam's apartment.

Cameron followed, already knowing they wouldn't find either Blake or Cam. His VW bus was nowhere to be seen, and there wasn't any light spilling out of the windows of the apartment.

Wanda pounded on the door a few times, and when no one answered, she called, "Cam? Blake? If you're in there, please open up. We just want to talk to you."

Nothing.

Wanda slumped against Cameron.

"Don't worry. We'll keep looking. Where did Blake say she was going?" he asked.

"To the cabins at the beach. Do you think they went there? Maybe they're camping out in his bus?" she speculated.

"All right. That's a start. First let's drive around town and see if we can spot Cam's bus. If not, we'll head to the coast. At least his vehicle is distinctive. It'll help on our search." Cameron wasn't convinced that they needed to wage an all-out search party for the teenagers. They were both competent enough to take care of themselves. He and Wanda could probably wait until the morning, see if either Blake or Cam called them back before heading to the coast, but he could tell that Wanda wasn't going to be able to sit at home by the phone. It wasn't in her nature to be patient, especially when she was worried. So he'd spend all night looking if that's what she wanted to do.

"That sounds like a plan." Before she got into his SUV, she wandered over to Gideon's house and peeked in the windows. After a moment, she shook her head and climbed into the passenger seat. "That was probably unnecessary since Cam's bus isn't here, but I had to check."

"I get it." Cam backed up and headed back to Main Street. If the kids were out for a night on the town, Cam's vehicle would be there somewhere. Though he doubted it. Blake wouldn't have made up a fake trip to the coast if they were just going to go out on a date. But they had to check just to be sure.

Twenty minutes later, it became clear that Cam's bus was not anywhere in town and they headed out to the coast. The thirty-mile drive that usually went by in a flash seemed to take hours. And by the time they pulled into the parking lot of the main campground office, Wanda had rattled off at least two dozen other campgrounds up and down the coast that they could also check before heading back to Keating Hollow.

Cameron prayed it didn't come to that.

There wasn't anyone manning the campground office, just instructions posted to find a site and drop payment into the lockbox. So Cameron rolled right into the grounds. Five minutes later they left, having only seen two campsites occupied and neither of them had a VW bus.

"Can we try the other campgrounds?" Wanda asked, sounding defeated.

"Sure. Which way?" Cameron asked as he idled at the exit of the campground.

"Left. There are half-a-dozen within twenty miles of each other."

Cameron made the turn and resigned himself to the fact that it was going to be a long night.

It was well past two in the morning when Cameron parked his SUV in Wanda's driveway. They'd searched every open campground within a sixty-mile radius and had come up empty. The trip to the coast had been a complete bust. And worse, neither Blake nor Cam had returned their calls.

"I can't believe this is happening," Wanda said, resting her head against the cool glass of the passenger window. "Why wouldn't she just tell me what she's up to?"

"Maybe she's scared of the consequences," Cameron said.

"What consequences?" Wanda asked. "I haven't punished her for anything. There aren't even that many rules, but no lying was definitely one of them. I don't get it."

"I don't mean punishment." He gave her a sympathetic smile. "I mean the consequences of how you'll feel about whatever it is she's doing. You're the only adult person in her life who is showing up for her. I'm sure she doesn't want to disappoint you and risk losing you, too."

"That's… maybe? I don't know." She sighed and climbed out of the SUV. Before she closed the door, she said, "Would you stay with me? I understand if you don't—"

"Yes," he said, cutting her off. He jumped out of his vehicle and followed her into the house. "Are you hungry? I could make you something to eat," he offered.

"No, not really. But feel free to grab something for

yourself. I'm going to go check Blake's room and see if there are any clues as to where she went."

Cameron watched her go and then went into her kitchen to grab a snack and something to drink. He hadn't actually eaten anything since lunch. After grabbing a granola bar and a bottle of water, he started up the stairs, and that's when he heard Wanda's cry of alarm. Cameron took the stairs two at a time and darted into Blake's room. "What is it?"

"All of her clothes are gone. Everything." She turned to him, her face chalk white. "The only thing she left was the sweatshirt I loaned her right after she moved in. She's gone, Cameron. She's run away."

Cameron placed his granola bar and water on Blake's dresser and folded Wanda up into his arms again. He held her close and murmured that they'd still find her. That they'd find out what happened. To not worry. They'd work it out. But deep inside, he was also freaking out. Cam had gone with her. Had he decided to skip town, too? Had his son, who'd just gotten a promotion and seemed so happy to meet his father and grandparents, run away with a girl he'd known for less than a month?

His heart started to race, and all of his empty words of comfort turned to dust on his tongue.

CAMERON WOKE with Wanda in his arms. It had taken some convincing, but after Wanda cried herself out while Cameron held her, he'd finally gotten her to agree to lay down with him. They'd both been fully clothed, and there hadn't been anything romantic about it. All he'd wanted to do was comfort her and make sure she knew she wasn't alone. It hadn't taken long for her to fall asleep, and he'd followed soon after.

The pale rays of the morning sun shone through one of her windows, illuminating her pretty face. She seemed so peaceful in her sleep, but he knew as soon as she woke those worry lines would be back.

After carefully extracting himself from her bed, he straightened his wrinkled clothes and went downstairs to rummage up some coffee. He was sitting on the front porch enjoying the quiet of the morning when Abby Townsend pulled into the driveway.

When she climbed out of her car, she was holding a squirmy golden puppy in her arms. Her expression was grim as she approached. "Any news?"

Cameron shook his head. "All of Blake's clothes are gone. She took everything."

Abby nodded. "Wanda texted me late last night with an update."

He nodded, remembering Wanda sending messages before she'd finally fallen asleep in his arms.

The puppy whined and tried to squirm out of Abby's grasp. "I thought Lyric might help a little," Abby said. "She and Wanda have gotten really close over the last week."

"Lyric. That's cute." He reached out and stroked the dog's head. "Congrats on the new addition. She's gorgeous."

"Oh, she's not mine. She's Wanda's. She rescued her from the mud down by the river during one of our golf cart races. I was watching her last night while you two were out searching for Blake." Abby held the puppy out to him.

He took the dog and cradled her in the crook of his arm. "Damn. I missed a lot, didn't I?"

"Not that much. And you're here now." She patted his arm

and added, "Let her know I came by and that if she needs me for anything to just call."

"I will. Thanks, Abby."

As Abby left, Cameron went back into the house, sat at the kitchen table with the puppy curled up in his lap, and started to make phone calls.

The call to Cam went straight to voice mail as expected. Then he called his parents. They hadn't heard from him and were distressed to hear he might have some hand in Blake's disappearance. The only one left to try was Hunter, Cam's boss.

Cameron didn't want to jeopardize his son's job in any way, so he'd need to be careful about what he said.

"Hunter McCormick," the man said when he answered.

"Hey, Hunter. This is Cameron Copeland, Cam's father?"

"Oh, right. Is everything with Cam's friend okay? I got a message last night that he wouldn't be into work today. We were planning on some overtime to get the kitchen finished in Gideon's house, but he said he had something come up. Something about a friend needing his help and that he'd be back in on Monday."

"Oh, well, that explains some things," Cameron lied. "I got a message from him, too, but the connection was bad, so I didn't get the gist. But you just cleared it up. Did he by chance say which friend or which town he was headed to? I need to get in touch with him, but I fear he isn't getting service on his phone."

"Only that he was headed out to the coast. Sorry, man. I don't have anything more specific than that. If I hear from him, I'll have him call you," Hunter said.

"You've been very helpful. Thanks, I appreciate it." Cameron ended the call and resigned himself to the fact that, unless Cam or Blake called, they were just going to have to wait until one or both of them showed up.

"No luck?" Wanda asked from the doorframe. She'd changed into fresh jeans and a sweatshirt. Her hair was still wet from the shower, and although her eyes looked tired, she was stunning with her rosy cheeks and full, naturally red lips.

He held his hand out to her as he shook his head. "No, but Abby brought someone by for you." He lifted the sleeping pup with his free hand. Lyric's eyes opened, and her tiny body started squirming as she desperately tried to get to her mistress.

Wanda's eyes misted as she took the puppy and snuggled her into her chest. "This is exactly who I needed." She stared at the ceiling and said, "Thanks, Abs."

CHAPTER 23

Wanda spent the entire weekend out in her yard prepping her beds for the planting season. It was still a little early in the season to plant anything, but there was no harm in weeding and churning the earth. By Monday morning, practically her entire backyard had been prepped for a summer garden, including new raised beds and planters for her windowsills.

She'd barely slept, even after exhausting herself, and that's why she was up and sitting on her porch at sunrise. Even Lyric hadn't gotten up with her. The puppy had stayed in bed with Cam, who hadn't gone home all weekend. He'd spent his time letting her work through her worry and anxiety while also keeping her fed and holding her together at night for the few hours of sleep she did manage to get.

It was almost frightening how hard Wanda was taking it that Blake had left. In just a few short weeks, she'd embraced her role as her sister's guardian and genuinely only wanted what was best for her. Running away with a boy at her age definitely wasn't in her best interest, and as more and more time went on, she started to blame Cam. What was he thinking, taking a minor away from her home? It was unforgivable.

She hadn't voiced her thoughts about Cam to Cameron of course. It was clear he had his own fears, wondering if his son was coming back to Keating Hollow. But he wouldn't have to wait much longer. It was Monday, the day Cam was supposed to be back at work. Soon enough, they'd know if he'd actually intended to make his stay in Keating Hollow permanent or not.

The orange glow of the rising sun started to peek over the mountain, and for the first time since Friday evening, Wanda felt a tiny moment of peace.

And that's when her phone rang.

Blake's smirking face flashed on the screen, making Wanda's heart leap into her throat. "Blake?" she said into the phone. "Where are you?"

"Wanda?"

"Cam? Is that you? Where's Blake?" And why was Cam calling and not her sister?

"She's here, with me," he said, and that's when she realized his voice was shaking.

"What happened?"

"We went to Red Bluff to meet her mother. It didn't go well. Blake has been in bed since Saturday afternoon, and I can't get her to get up. She's refusing to come home. Honestly, Wanda, I'm really worried. She won't let me help her. She won't eat. I don't know what to do."

"Her mother? Karen? That doesn't make any sense. Her mother doesn't live in California," Wanda said.

"I don't know about any of that, but Blake saw her on Saturday. She didn't tell me all of the details, but from what

I've put together, it seems Blake thought her mom wanted her back and that they were getting an apartment together. But it was all a lie. Her mom only wanted money."

Nausea rolled through Wanda at the thought of Karen Danvers using Blake like that. The nausea was quickly followed by pure rage. If Karen ever crossed Wanda's path again, the woman was going to live to regret it. "Cam, give me the address where you are. Cameron and I will be there as soon as we can."

WANDA'S NERVES were completely shot by the time Cameron pulled his SUV into the tiny motel's parking lot. The drive to Red Bluff from Keating Hollow had been an excruciating two and a half hours of winding road. It made her sick to realize that because Red Bluff was in the exact opposite direction of the coast, Wanda and Cameron never would've found them if Cam hadn't called.

"This is where they've been?" Wanda asked as she clutched the bag of potions she'd picked up from the healer on the way out of town. The two-story motel looked to have been built back in the sixties, and if Wanda had to guess, that was the last time it had been painted, too. Debris was scattered in the parking lot, and there were a couple of broken-down cars near the dumpster that probably hadn't moved since nineteen eighty-nine.

"It's probably where Karen had them meet her," Cameron said.

Wanda nodded and stuck close to him as they climbed the cement stairs.

"Hey, pretty lady. Got any candy for me?" a guy with long

hair and an even longer beard called from the doorway of the motel room right in front of them.

"Back off, jackass. She's a fire witch, so if you don't want to get your ass toasted, you'll behave yourself," Cameron said.

"Fire witch. Badass." He gave Wanda an approving glance but stepped back into his room and closed the door before they reached him.

"I've never toasted anyone's ass before," Wanda said. "Whooped some ass, yes. Toasted, no."

Cameron chuckled and squeezed her hand. "Sometimes subtlety does the trick just fine."

"Subtlety isn't my strong suit," Wanda countered, recognizing that she was talking nonsense just to keep some of her sanity.

"This is it," Cameron said, stopping at room 212.

Wanda stepped up and knocked.

The door swung open and Cam appeared, relief flashing all over his haggard features the moment he saw them. "Thank the gods," he breathed. "She's just inside."

Wanda didn't hesitate. She swept past him and entered the orange and brown room. There was a stale, musty smell in the air, and Wanda couldn't help but wonder how the place passed any sort of health inspections. It clearly hadn't been updated in decades, and the likelihood of mold in the walls was something she didn't want to contemplate.

"Blake?" she said the moment she saw her sister curled up in the fetal position on one of the beds. She wore sweats and a T-shirt, but it was clear that, just like Cam had said, she hadn't moved in a while. There were remnants of makeup smeared under her eyes, and her hair was sticking out in all directions.

Her sister didn't move or even seem to register that Wanda was there.

Wanda pulled an anti-depressant potion out of her bag that the healer had recommended for emergency situations and crawled on the bed to sit right next to Blake. The scents of lavender and stale sweat assaulted her nose, and Wanda tried to remember to breathe through her mouth.

"Hey, sweetie. I have something for you to drink, okay?" Wanda coaxed as she stroked Blake's cheek with her thumb. "Think you can do that for me?"

Her sister at least looked her way, confirming that she must've heard her.

Wanda twisted the cap off, shoved a straw into the bottle, and then held the straw close to Blake's mouth. "You need to drink this, Blake."

No response.

"Okay, you don't have to. But if you don't, we're going to have no choice but to take you to the emergency room, and then neither of us will have any control over what happens until there's a full evaluation."

Blake's eyes sought hers again.

"Are you ready to try now?"

Blake opened her mouth just enough so that Wanda could insert the straw. She waited until her sister got at least a quarter of the potion down.

"That's enough for now," Wanda said, replacing the top. "We're going to take you home now, okay, sweetie?"

Tears filled Blake's eyes, and she gave her sister a tiny nod.

Wanda waved Cameron over. "Can you carry her to the SUV? Cam and I will gather their things."

"Sure." He kissed Wanda on the top of her head and then

scooped Blake up into his arms, all while murmuring those same soothing words he'd whispered to Wanda when she'd been so upset about Blake being missing.

After Cameron and Blake disappeared out of the motel room, Wanda turned to Cam. "Is everything packed up?"

He nodded and opened the closet. Blake's two suitcases were in there along with a backpack. Cam slung the backpack on and carried both of the suitcases himself.

"I can help," Wanda said.

"No. I've got them. Really, it's the least I can do." Then he glanced at the threadbare chair in the corner of the room. "But if you can grab her purse and shoes, that would be great."

Wanda nodded, searched the room for anything else they might have left behind, and then hurried to catch up with Cameron and Blake.

Cam stood beside the SUV, his hands shoved in his pockets as he watched Cameron deposit Blake into the backseat. "It's my fault," he said quietly. "I never should have agreed to drive her here."

Wanda placed Blake's things in the back of the SUV and then turned to Cam. "Why *did* you drive her here? Did you know that she was planning to leave Keating Hollow permanently?"

His eyes widened. "No way. I would've tried to talk her out of it, and I'm pretty sure she knew that. It's why she didn't tell you. She didn't want to hear that she shouldn't trust her mom. As for why I brought her here, she was going to do it with or without me, and I just couldn't stand the thought of her coming here by herself, considering her history with her mom. I just wanted to be here to protect her and then bring her home on Sunday." He let out a bitter laugh. "You can see how well that turned out."

"So you were watching out for her?" That was something Wanda could believe. She also hadn't forgotten that as soon as things got bad, he'd called her immediately.

"Yes. I'm so sorry, Wanda. I don't want to be that guy who's a bad influence. I just want her safe. I was hoping once she saw her mom she'd get some closure, or answers, or hell, I don't know. I just couldn't let her see her mom by herself."

Wanda gently squeezed his shoulder. "Don't beat yourself up. I know how stubborn and independent she is. I appreciate that you were trying to protect her. Thank you."

He hung his head. "There's nothing to thank me for. I'm sorry she lied to you and that I was a participant."

"You took care of her. I'm grateful." Wanda opened the door to the back of the SUV and slid in beside her sister.

Blake turned to look at her through sad eyes. Her tears started to fall, and she whispered, "She doesn't love me."

"Aw, sweetie." Wanda wrapped her arm around Blake's shoulder and gave her a long hug.

Blake's body shook with her sobs, and eventually, she laid her head on Wanda's lap, clutching one of her hands in both of hers. "I'm sorry."

"Shhh. Don't worry about that now. I understand why you came. It's okay. Let's just get you home, and we'll go from there. Everything is okay now. You're safe. You're loved. I promise." Wanda smoothed Blake's hair for the entire two and a half hours back to Keating Hollow.

By the time Cam pulled into Wanda's driveway, her sister was sound asleep. Wanda gave him a hopeful smile. "Any chance you can carry her inside?"

He let out a soft chuckle. "I'm on it. Where do you want her? Couch? Her bedroom?"

"Better take her upstairs," Wanda said.

Once they had Blake and all of her luggage in the house and tucked away upstairs, Wanda walked with Cameron to the front door.

"Thank you for… everything you've done for us these last few days. Honestly, I'm not sure how I would've held up without you," Wanda said.

Cameron brushed a lock of hair out of her eyes and said, "I think you would've been okay, but thank you for allowing me to take care of you. I know that's not exactly your strong suit."

It was Wanda's turn to chuckle. "It really isn't. But I like it when you're here. Maybe after everything settles down, you'll let me take you to dinner as a thank you?"

"Did Wanda Danvers just ask me on a date?" His eyes were wide as he feigned shock.

"I believe she did. But Cameron Copeland hasn't answered yet."

"Oh, I thought the answer was obvious. Yes. It's always a yes when it comes to you." He brought his hand up and cupped her cheek with his palm. "Call me if you need anything, okay? Dinner. Chocolate. A foot rub. I'll come right over."

Damn, he was way too good to her, and she knew it. "Cameron," she said, staring at his lips.

"Yes?"

"Right now I just need you to kiss me like you mean it," she whispered.

"Done." He leaned down, covered her mouth with his, and

took his time worshiping her lips, savoring her taste, and teasing her tongue.

By the time he pulled back, her entire body was tingling from his touch, and her heart was nearly pounding right out of her chest. She'd completely lost herself in him, and for once, that didn't have her running scared. "That was perfect."

He smiled at her, kissed her one last time, and then said, "I'll talk to you soon, Wanda."

She watched him climb into his SUV and pull out into the street. It wasn't until the taillights of his SUV disappeared around the corner that she shut the door and headed back upstairs to keep an eye on her sister.

CHAPTER 24

It had been four days since Wanda had brought Blake home. They still hadn't really talked about what happened in Red Bluff. Blake had brought it up once, but she'd immediately started sobbing again. Wanda told her they didn't need to talk about it right now and that all she wanted was for Blake to get better.

They'd been working on it. First, Wanda called Gerry Whipple, one of the town healers. She'd made a house call and determined that other than a little dehydration Blake was physically fine, but that she really need to see a mental health professional. She gave Wanda the business card of someone she recommended highly for teenagers, and Wanda got Blake in immediately. She'd gone to the therapy three days in a row, and today was the first day she'd driven herself.

Wanda was waiting at home, trying to help Blake earn back both her trust and some independence. It wasn't easy though. Wanda kept looking at the clock and calculating how long it took to get from the therapy office in Eureka and back home. By Wanda's calculation, Blake should've arrived seven minutes ago.

Tick. Tick. Tick. Wanda couldn't take her eyes off the clock while she drummed her fingernails on the kitchen table. When another minute went by, Wanda got to her feet and moved into the kitchen. If she didn't do something to keep busy, she was going to lose what was left of her mind.

Twenty minutes later, when Blake finally walked into the house, Wanda was elbow deep in a double batch of sugar cookies.

"Wanda? I'm home," Blake called as she walked through the house. Lyric barked and ran into the living room to greet her.

Wanda didn't reply for fear she would snap at her sister. She was thirty minutes late coming back from her appointment, and while normally that wouldn't have been a problem, things were different now. Wanda's trust had been broken, and while Blake seemed to be doing better, Wanda couldn't be sure when or if she'd have another breakdown. Any deviation from routine sent Wanda's anxiety through the roof.

"There you are," Blake said, striding in with a smile on her face. "Cookies? Need help?"

"No thanks. I've got it." Wanda went back to dropping little balls of dough on the cookie sheets and willed herself to relax. The puppy returned to the kitchen and sat expectantly at Wanda's feet. Wanda glanced down at her. "You know you don't get cookies."

Blake stood there for a minute and then walked into the kitchen and started loading the dishwasher.

Wanda watched her sister in her peripheral vision. It wasn't that Blake wasn't usually helpful with chores around the house. She had been before the Red Bluff incident, but since they'd been home, she'd spent most of her time in her room. This new behavior appeared to be some sort of progress.

Wanda slid the tray of cookies into the oven and set the timer. Then she poured herself a glass of wine and headed for the living room with Lyric trotting behind her. The little doodle had become Wanda's constant shadow.

"Can we talk?" Blake called after her.

Wanda froze and then slowly turned around. She cleared her throat. "About?"

Blake's face flushed. She glanced around, avoiding Wanda's gaze as she waved a hand. "Everything. Me. What happened."

"All right," Wanda said and slowly walked back into the kitchen. She took a seat at the table and waited. It wasn't long before Lyric curled up at her feet.

Blake sat across from her and clasped her hands together. "First off, I know I already told you I'm sorry for what I did, but I need to say it again. I'm sorry, Wanda. I lied to you, worried you, and was prepared to leave without saying goodbye. It was selfish and cowardly, and you didn't deserve that."

It was on the tip of Wanda's tongue to excuse her sister's behavior, but she held back. She already knew part of her sister's therapy sessions were focused on Blake learning to take responsibility for her actions and to not blame her parents. "Okay. Thank you for saying that."

Blake nodded and finally met her gaze. Tears welled in her dark eyes, but she blinked them back. "I need you to know that I didn't want to leave *you*. I just wanted my mom to want *me*."

"I know, honey," Wanda said and reached out to cover Blake's hand with her own. "But thank you for telling me that, too. You know all I want is what's best for you."

"Mom and Dad aren't what's best for me. That's why I didn't tell you."

The pain in her voice nearly broke Wanda in two. She wished with all of her heart that she could absorb Blake's wounds from the years of neglect and abandonment so that her sister didn't have to keep reliving that pain. She knew that was what the therapy was for and that Blake would push through it, but that didn't stop Wanda from wanting to make it easier for her. "I know that, too," Wanda said with a tiny smile.

Blake placed both palms on the table and took a deep breath. "I'm working on my trust issues in therapy."

Wanda nodded. That was expected. With her unstable upbringing, she had a lot to work through.

"My therapist thinks I should tell you what happened with my mother."

"What do *you* want to do?" Wanda asked. She did not want Blake to feel like she was forced to talk to her. As much as she desperately wanted to know what Karen had put her through, she didn't want Blake to have to relive it if she wasn't up to it. After seeing Blake so thoroughly broken, Wanda would do just about anything to keep her from going back to that dark place.

"I need you to know because there is a one hundred percent chance that she is going to try to use me again, and I'm going to need someone I can talk to who understands."

"Cam isn't that person?" Wanda asked, only because he was the one whom she'd confided in this time.

Blake smiled at the mention of his name. "Cam is great,

but he hasn't experienced what we have. His mom never left him willingly. And his dad… well, he didn't even know he had one, but the minute they met they were like besties or something. His luck in the parent department is far superior to ours."

Wanda couldn't help but chuckle at that. "True. Okay, I'm ready. Walk me through it."

"You know when you got me my smart phone and mom left me a message after I sent an update to all of my contacts?"

"Yeah. You didn't seem interested in talking to her after that," Wanda said.

"I couldn't help it. I called her the next day, and she was sweet, like she can be sometimes. She said she missed me and that she and Dad weren't together anymore. Over the next few days, she told me all about an apartment she was going to rent in Red Bluff. That she had a job at a restaurant there. That she wanted me to move in with her so we could start over. It all sounded like she was really trying. She told me that if I could cover the deposit she had enough to get it rented." Her voice broke on the word rented.

Wanda was silently fuming, but she didn't want to blow up in the middle of the story. This was something Blake needed to get out. She squeezed Blake's hand just to let her know she had support.

"She kept pressing me. She knew I had a job because I'd told her about it, and in retrospect, that was the moment when she started setting me up to take my money. She told me she was living at a shelter and that the sooner I got there, the sooner she'd have a safe place to be. She had a lot of stories, and I was really torn up about it. Finally, I just made the decision to go. Cam wouldn't let me go by myself. I didn't even know for sure if I planned to stay. I took my clothes, because if she really had changed, I kind of felt like I needed to be there for her. But of course when I got there, it was all a lie. She just wanted my cash. Told me her new boyfriend wouldn't want me around."

Blake wiped at her eyes and then continued. "She actually pushed me and told me to go before he saw me because otherwise I'd be expected to…" Her face crumbled, and the tears flowed harder. It took her a moment to get herself under control. When she continued, her voice was hard and full of pure steel. "I told her I'd kill him first, and that's when she slapped me. I left then and didn't look back. By the time I got back to the motel, I was numb and just fell into bed, and you know the rest."

Wanda couldn't take it anymore. She gently pulled her feet out from under Lyric's warm body, got up, walked around to the other side of the table, and pulled her sister into her arms. "You deserve so much better than Karen can give you, sweet girl," Wanda whispered. "I'm proud of you for standing up for yourself. And also for having empathy for a woman who has spent most of her life battling drugs. She needs help, but you don't owe her anything. It doesn't need to be you. The next time she pulls this—and we both know she will—you'll have to tools to deal with her. And if it gets hard, you come to me. We'll work it out together. Do you hear me?"

Blake nodded and held onto her sister with everything she had. Eventually she sobbed out, "I'm so sorry for making you worry."

"I'm sorry you've had to deal with so much from the woman who is supposed to love and protect you."

They held each other tightly, and when Wanda finally

pulled back, she stared Blake in the eye and said, "I love you. I understand what happened, and there's nothing to forgive. I let it go the minute you were safely back in this house. Just promise me one thing, will you?"

"What's that?"

Wanda squeezed her sister's hands and said, "I just want us to be honest with each other. Without that, we have no trust. And I think trust is just about the most important thing to both of us, don't you?"

"Yes." She nodded earnestly.

"Then right here, right now, we both promise that no matter what, we'll have honesty between us."

Blake held her pinky finger up. Wanda grinned and wrapped her pinky around Blake's.

"On three?" Wanda asked.

Blake nodded, and when Wanda counted to three, they both said, "I promise."

Afterward they both laughed.

The buzzer sounded for the cookies, and still chuckling, Wanda went to retrieve them from the oven.

Blake, followed by Lyric, joined her while Wanda transferred the cookies to a cooling rack. "So, in the name of honesty, what's going on with you and Cameron?"

Wanda let out a startled laugh. She hadn't been expecting that question. "I don't know. I guess we were seeing each other and now…" She shrugged. "Life has been a little hectic. We'll see."

"Can I just say one thing about that and then let it alone?" Blake asked.

"Uh, okay." Did she really want to hear this? She wasn't sure, but they had just pledged they'd be honest, so here was the first test, she supposed.

"I heard you telling Cameron that you didn't think it was a good time to be dating because you needed to be focusing on me. And I just want to go on record in saying that I like him and you together. He's a great guy as far as I can tell. You should go for it."

Wanda shook her head, amused at this turn in the conversation. "Really? You think dating someone who lives in another city is a good idea?"

"First of all, he's moving here. Cam told me yesterday. And second of all, yes. Why do you think I invited him over that one night?"

"Which night?"

"The one when I told you I'd been deleting spam off your phone after spilling the beans about Cameron being his son. Oops." She grimaced. "That was another lie. But the only one as far as I know."

"You invited him over? Really?" Wanda asked, remembering that night. They'd sat in her living room and talked a lot. She'd had a really nice time with him.

"Really." Blake smirked. "Now go tell him you want to be his girlfriend or something, because that man is at least half in love with you already. And you deserve someone like him in your life." She grabbed two cookies, winked, and looked down at the puppy as she said, "Let's go Lyric. We have some playing to do."

CHAPTER 25

Cameron sat at his desk in the downstairs apartment of his parents' rental and stared at the blank page of the script he was supposed to be writing. It had been weeks since he'd gotten any real work done. Between flying back and forth from Keating Hollow and Vancouver, his muse had really just left the building.

Or it had when he was working on ideas for *Fire Valley*.

But when he was working on his passion project that revolved around a fiery redhead in a small magical town… That was when the ideas really came out to play.

Frustrated that the words weren't coming for the project he was supposed to be working on, he clicked out of *Fire Valley* and switched to *Muse of the Witch*. Instantly he felt lighter and started working on a touching scene between the protagonist and her younger sister who'd recently reconnected after being apart for a number of years.

His fingers flew over the keys as the words just poured out of him. He didn't know how long he'd been sitting there, but when he finally finished the chapter when the heroine meets her hero, he sat back and took a look at his word count.

Over four thousand words in just three hours.

And it felt glorious to be back in the saddle again, even if it wasn't work that was contracted… yet. He had a feeling he wouldn't have too much trouble placing it, and if he did, he'd find a way to produce it himself.

He got up to stretch and heard a knock at his door. He assumed it was one of his parents dropping by to let him know they were heading somewhere on their way out. They did that often. Running a hand through his unruly hair, he strode to the door and was shocked into silence when he found Wanda standing there in form-fitting jeans and a silky red blouse that did a fabulous job of showing off her ample cleavage.

"Hey," he said, feeling a goofy smile claim his lips as he held the door open for her. "What brings you by today?"

She held up a plastic container he hadn't even noticed she was holding. "I baked cookies. Thought you might like some."

"Cookies?" he asked. What the hell was wrong with him? He'd just written a fabulous meet-cute in his script, and yet, here he was fumbling his lines like an idiot.

"Yes, cookies." She laughed. "Can I come in or are you going to make me stand out here all day?"

"Oh! Right." He chuckled as he waved her in. "Sorry. I was just so surprised to see you that I'm obviously off my game."

She placed a hand on his chest as she swept by him and blew him a kiss. "I'm sure you'll recover quickly."

His heart melted and turned into a pile of goo at his feet. This was the Wanda he'd first been attracted to. Flirty, confident, fun. But now he knew her to be a caring, well-rounded individual with a giant heart as well, and he was all in. He just needed to convince her he was worth it.

She stood in his little apartment, taking in his large bed in the corner, the built-in office, and small sitting area. It wasn't large, but it was bathed in light from the floor-to-ceiling windows and had a wonderful view of the valley.

When she turned around to look at him, he blurted, "You were right."

She raised a curious eyebrow. "About?"

"That fight we had at your house that day, when I said I wanted more…" he started. Her eyes widened and flashed with panic at his words. He hurried to finish his explanation so she wouldn't think he was overstepping again. "You said I was pushing you when you weren't ready. And you were right. You have so much going on with your sister, and I don't want to cause you any more stress. I want to be the one who helps you unwind. So, I just wanted to say that I'm still all in, but I'm going to wait patiently until you're ready. No pushing. No expectations. But I'll still be here."

Her lips curved up into a smile, and her eyes twinkled with what he could only assume was happiness. She just looked radiant, and it took everything he had to not move in and kiss her. This was a conversation they had to have.

"I heard you're moving here to Keating Hollow. Cam told Blake, and Blake told me. Is this going to be your permanent pad, or are you going to look for something a little bigger… and maybe a little more private?"

He eyed her, wondering what she was up to. He knew that tone in her voice. It was the one she got right before she started shucking his clothes off. "What's going on here?"

She laughed and moved in to press both palms on his

chest. "I'm flirting with you. Has it been so long that you forgot the cues?"

"No, but I am wondering about this change in direction. I did just tell you that I'm backing off because I don't want to rush you, and yet…" He glanced at the bed, already aching to get her into it.

She chuckled again. "Sorry, you just look so good when you're in writer mode. I think it's the crazy hair. It means you've been creating, and I love that."

"Wanda," he said with a groan. "You're killing me here."

She moved in closer and stared him in the eye when she said, "I came over here today to tell you that I was wrong."

"You?"

"Yep, me. I was using Blake as an excuse to keep you at arm's length. The truth is I'm crazy about you but scared out of my mind. Blake isn't the only one with abandonment issues. My dad left us when I was very young, and my mom worked hard just to keep a roof over our heads. Then she was taken from me too soon. Since she never had a successful relationship, I guess I got it in my head that it wasn't something I should do either."

Cameron wanted to pull her into a hug and tell her that he'd never hurt or disappoint her, but he knew better. She had things to say, and he meant to let her. Besides, he couldn't make those promises. The best he could do was promise to love and respect her. "I get that. Your examples haven't exactly instilled confidence."

"Even Lin Townsend, my pseudo-father, had his marriage fall apart, and he's the best man I know. But I have to remember that he's been with Clair for over fifteen years. And then there are the Pelshes, and your parents, and hell, most of my friends. They are all happily married. Why not me, too?"

"You want to get married?" he challenged, just because he couldn't help himself.

"If you're going to be standing at the alter with me, I'd consider it," she said, throwing out her own challenge.

He laughed. "Oh, I better be the one beside you at the altar, otherwise I'd have some major ass kicking to do."

She pressed up on her toes and gave him a soft kiss.

Cameron instantly wrapped his arms around her and pulled her in tight against his body. "What did we just decide?"

"We're engaged, obviously," she said, her lips twitching in amusement.

"Don't say that unless you mean it, Wanda. 'Cause I'm not playing around. I'm going on record here and laying it all on the line. I'm in love with you."

She stared at him with her mouth open in real surprise this time.

"I know you weren't expecting me to say that," he said, brushing a lock of hair out of her eyes. "And I'm still not pressuring you. I said it because I meant it, not because I'm expecting—"

"I love you, too, you big rambling goof. I love you, and that's what I came here to tell you." She flung her arms around him again, and this time when they kissed, both of them were all in.

When they finally came up for air, he frowned down at her. "So, does this really mean we're engaged? I kinda thought I'd do a much better job at proposing."

She chuckled. "How about we just go with we're

exclusively dating? And maybe think about moving in together before we talk about engagements? But only if it's not here. I adore your parents, but I'm not living in their house."

"Does this mean I can call you my girlfriend now?" he asked, needling her.

"You'd better if you don't want my size nine up your backside," she said.

"Finally." He grabbed her hand and said, "Come on. I have something to show you."

"Oh? What?" she asked as she followed him to the white Jeep that sat in his driveway.

"I turned in the rental and bought this. What do you think?" he asked.

"Does the top come off?" she asked.

"Of course."

"Then it's perfect."

Wanda studied him the entire ride down the mountain and to the edge of town, just past the Townsend property and onto the acreage she'd always wanted but hadn't thought she could handle on her own. "I heard your parents were thinking about buying this land to start a farm," she said.

"They did and they are, but that's only part of the news." He took the Jeep off the dirt road and through a pasture until he got to a section of land that was part redwoods with a small meadow that overlooked a running brook. The Jeep came to a stop, and he asked, "What do you think?"

"It's gorgeous. In fact, I always kind of thought that if I had enough nerve to take on ten acres this is exactly where I'd put my house."

Cameron nodded. "Yeah. Me, too. Want to come with me when I have the plans drawn up?"

"What? This land is yours? I thought your parents were the buyers."

Cameron jumped out of the Jeep and jogged over to her side, opening her door before she had a chance and then helping her out into the field. "My parents were planning to buy it, but it turned out that while they had enough for the land, they didn't have enough capital to start the farm. So I partnered with them under the condition that I could build our house here."

Wanda tore her gaze from the brook to stare at him. "You said *our* house."

"I did," he said. "I'd like to build the house of your dreams right here, Wanda Danvers, and then I want to date you for however long it takes until you're ready to be my wife."

"How is this happening?" she asked, her voice full of wonder. "This is not what I expected when I showed up at your door today."

"Oh, yeah? What did you expect?"

She shrugged. "Oh, I don't know. To apologize, have my way with you, and then leave with the knowledge that I finally had a boyfriend that I intend to keep."

"You can still have your way with me," he said, pulling her closer to the trees. "There's no one out here but you and me and maybe a few deer."

Wanda grinned up at him and said, "Careful what you wish for."

"Oh, I've been very careful," he growled and tugged her toward him. "Very careful indeed."

Laughing, Wanda broke free and ran closer to the trees. Cameron chased her and tackled her to the ground, where they remained entangled in each other for most of the afternoon.

CHAPTER 26

"Are you ready for this?" Cameron asked his son as they stood outside Incantation Café.

"As ready as I'll ever be, I guess." Cam clutched the birthday card Jessie had sent him many years ago and pulled the door to the coffee shop open.

Cameron followed his son inside and spotted a couple he knew must be Jessie and her significant other right away. They were sitting at a table in the far corner, a fair distance away from the other customers. It was a good spot for a little privacy.

"Cam?" The taller, thin woman with short silver hair jumped up from her chair and opened her arms wide as if Cam was supposed to throw himself into them.

"Jessie!" Cam's entire face lit up with joy as he rushed over and gave the woman a giant bear hug. He lifted her up and spun her around easily then gently placed her back on her feet. "I can't believe you're here."

"Neither can I," she said, wiping a lone tear from her cheek. "I honestly thought I'd never see you again." Jessie turned to Cameron and said in a teasing tone, "You must be the mythical Cameron Copeland."

"Mythical?" Cameron asked as he shook her hand.

"That's what Tori used to call you," she said, giving him a sad smile. "I'm so sorry. I really tried to get her to contact you. It was a real point of contention between us."

"So you knew," Cam said, his expression darkening with frustration.

"I knew," Jessie confirmed and then led them to her table. "Cameron, Cam, this is my partner, Trish."

Trish was shorter and curvier than Jessie with dark wavy hair that was pulled back into a long braid. "Hello. It's nice to finally meet you both." She hugged Cam, and then when she turned to Cameron, he thought she was going to shake his hand, but instead she went in for the hug and said, "Sorry. I can't help it. I'm a hugger."

He chuckled. "It's all good. I come from a long line of them."

They all took a seat and silence settled around them. After a few beats, Cameron got up and said, "Does anyone need anything? I'm going to get a coffee. Cam?"

"Large mocha, extra whip," he said.

"Oh, we're fine." Jessie waved to the cups already on the table.

Cameron nodded. "You guys go ahead and catch up. I'll be back in a few." After he ordered, Cameron stood at the end of the bar watching Cam interact with Jessie. He was smiling while she and her partner took turns telling a story, and eventually they all started laughing.

He'd thought he'd be resentful or have a twinge of jealousy seeing his son with someone he didn't know who'd had a major part in Cam's childhood. Instead, all he felt was grateful that Cam had reconnected with someone he'd loved and trusted, even if it had been for a relatively short time. When the drinks were ready, he returned to the table and was quiet while the three chatted about Jessie and Trish's life together.

The couple lived on the north shore in Tahoe, and they worked as ski instructors in the winter and ran a charter sailboat in the summer. Cameron was impressed. It sounded like a wonderful, mostly laid-back life where they got to do what they loved every day.

"What about you, Cameron?" Trish asked. "What do you do?"

His eyebrows shot up in surprise. He figured if Jessie knew about him when Cam was a child that they probably also knew he'd written a hit screenplay when he was fresh out of college. His career had taken off from there. "I'm a writer."

Cam rolled his eyes. "He's a screenwriter. He has a movie and a television series he co-wrote with Miranda Moon in production right now."

"Screenwriter?" Jessie said, surprised. "Tori told me you were a starving artist. She made it sound like you were selling paintings down at the Santa Monica pier."

Cameron barked out a laugh. "That sounds like Tori. She never was impressed with my career ambitions. She thought it was impractical."

"Impractical," Jessie said with a nod. "Just like being a ski instructor. It was a long-term stretch goal of mine to get to a point where I could live the life I do now, but Tori always turned up her nose at it. She always said skiing and sailing weren't real jobs."

Trish shook her head sadly. "It's too bad she couldn't

relate to other people's dreams. What do you think that was about?"

"She wanted to be an artist herself," Cameron said. "Her father refused to pay her tuition unless she majored in something practical. That's why she was studying accounting. Did she finish and become an accountant?"

"Yep," Jessie confirmed and took a sip of her drink. "She hated it, too. But I never knew she wanted to be an artist. I knew she had some skills. She drew some portraits of Cam when he was young." Jessie dug around in a canvas bag and retrieved a wallet. With a flick of her wrist, she produced a wallet-sized portrait of a child about five years old.

"This is Cam?" Cameron asked, in awe of the detail. "It's incredible."

"It really is. This was made from a photo of you, Cam. I loved it so much, your mom did this for me."

"Wow," he said. "She really was talented. Though, I look like a complete dork, and I question your taste for loving this so much. But I guess I can overlook it. You did drive all the way over here from Tahoe."

They sat together, sharing stories for a little over an hour before Cam became impatient and finally asked, "Why didn't she ever tell me about my dad?"

The table went completely silent, and all the lightheartedness they'd shared vanished.

Finally, Jessie cleared her throat and said, "I think she was afraid."

"Of what?"

Jessie clasped her hand over his. "That you'd want to meet him and that you would no longer be all hers."

Cameron's stomach rolled with nausea as he finally began

to understand what had gone wrong with his relationship with Tori.

"All hers? I'm not a thing. I'm a person," Cam scoffed.

"We know that," Jessie said, soothingly. "She knew that, too, but prior to having you, her life revolved around what other people wanted for her. Her dad had his ideas. Cameron had his. Even her grandparents had stipulations on what she could do with the small inheritance they'd left her. She felt like she had to earn the love of everyone in her life, except for you. You loved her no matter what she did. You didn't care if she was an accountant or not. Or where she lived, or who she dated. You just loved her. And she craved that."

Prior to this revelation, learning that Tori thought she had to earn his love would've wounded Cameron badly. But he saw it now. She'd been forever trying to turn herself inside out to please other people. And Cameron, without realizing it, had become the wedge between her and her family. He'd always encouraged her to pursue her art, but if she did that, she'd piss off her father. And not pursuing art probably made her feel like she was disappointing Cameron. But that still didn't explain why she didn't tell him about the pregnancy.

Was Jessie right? Had Tori thought he'd take her child away? A cold chill ran down his spine at the thought. Cameron never would've done that.

"Cameron?"" Jessie said.

"Huh?"

"Are you okay?" she asked.

He blinked and nodded. "Just processing what you've said and maybe understanding some things better."

"The bottom line is that Tori was afraid of what she really wanted. She was attracted to passionate dreamers who were pursuing their lives on their own terms, and any time one of us would get close to pushing her to do the same, she ran. That's what she did to your dad, Cam, and a few others before I entered the picture. I'm sure she would've done the same to me if we'd lasted any longer. Instead, she kicked me out because I didn't agree with her choices."

Jessie paused to take a long sip of water and then continued. "As for not telling you, Cameron, she said she didn't even know she was pregnant for a few months and by then she was terrified to face you because of the way she left. Then she just put her head in the sand and decided that matter was settled."

"That all sounds very much like Tori," Cameron said. "I'm not sure I'm ever going to be okay about missing Cam's childhood, but I can say that I'm glad Cam had you in his life for a short period of time. You obviously love him. So thank you for watching out for him. I appreciate it."

Cam gave his dad a sideways hug and then went back to talking to Jessie. That's when he learned she'd been sending him birthday and Christmas cards every year since she'd left. Jessie only learned of his mother's passing when his last birthday card was returned.

"Every year?" Cam echoed. "Every year and she kept them from me." He ran a frustrated hand through his hair. "That's some next-level BS right there. Wow."

"I'm sorry, Cam," Jessie said. "It kills me to know you thought I left you, too. But I never did. I carry you with me everywhere I go." She tapped a finger on her wallet. "In here and in my heart."

It wasn't long after that when they said their goodbyes to the lovely couple from the Sierra's. Jessie and Trish vowed to come back again in the summer to spend some time with Cam.

"I'm already looking forward to it," Cam said, but the light had gone out of his eyes. He was upset. And who could blame him? He'd learned a lot about his mother, stuff she couldn't even defend. It was a lot to take in.

"Are you all right?" Cameron asked him as they exited the café.

"Not really, but I will be. I always knew she marched to the beat of her own drum. And honestly, what did I expect? That there was some magical version of the story where my mother didn't look like the bad guy? She kept us apart for her own selfish reasons. It's unforgivable."

Cameron had to agree. "That's true, but you can find acceptance. That's all we can hope for. So take some time to feel everything you're feeling and then try to move past it. It's all you can do."

Cam eyed his father. "You seem… more settled. Did something about that conversation help you?"

"Absolutely. I finally understand why she did what she did. And now I can stop asking myself what *I* did wrong. The answer is nothing. And neither did you, Son. Remember that."

Cam nodded thoughtfully. When they got into the Jeep, Cam looked at his father. "You know what, Dad?"

"What's that?"

"I love you."

Cameron beamed at him. "I love you, too. Now let's get out of here and go find the Danvers sisters. We have a wedding to go to."

CHAPTER 27

Amelia Holiday picked at the wedding cake and tried not to look like she was ready to drown herself in the champagne fountain. Could there be anything worse than being forced to attend a wedding on Valentine's Day when you were both single and pregnant?

Your ex could be here. That would be worse, the helpful voice in her head said.

"Shut it," she muttered, praying she hadn't just jinxed herself.

Grayson Riley. How was it that the guy she'd had a hot affair with for a few months in Cape Cod had ended up in Keating Hollow of all places? She knew she was a coward. That day he'd been looking for her in the Enchanted K Gallery, she'd panicked. She never should've hidden behind the counter. It had been the perfect opportunity to break her news, but she'd been completely unprepared.

Now she was going to have to track him down, and considering she never wanted to see him again, that was something she'd gladly put off as long as possible.

She glanced up, trying to focus on anything other than thoughts of Grayson, and took in the gorgeous magically enhanced decorations. They were at the Pelsh family winery, likely because it was the only venue large enough for an inside wedding where practically the entire town was in attendance. That also meant they had access to all of the powerful witches in town, and they had gone all out.

In the center of each table, there were candles with flames that flickered through various pictures of Shannon and Brian. They ranged from when they were both kids right up until present day, and the images told a story about their journeys in life. Ice sculptures in the shape of Cupid had come to life after the ceremony and were randomly shooting their harmless arrows at people on the dance floor. But Amelia's absolute favorite enchantment was the customized chocolate bar. All you had to do was think about what kind of chocolate you wanted, and it appeared out of thin air.

"Amelia!" What are you doing back here all by yourself?" Hanna Pelsh asked, moving toward her with a champagne bottle in her hand.

"Just taking a breather," Amelia said, waving a hand toward the dance floor. "Rex spun me around so many times, I think I'll still be twirling when my head hits the pillow tonight."

"Your brother is an excellent dancer. Did he study as a kid?" Hanna asked.

"Nope. I think he and Holly might be taking ballroom lessons though. She said she has a list she's working through, like forty things to do before you turn forty or something like that. And Rex is so over the moon about her that he just indulges her every whim."

"That's right, he does." Holly flopped down in the chair beside Amelia. "Hey, Hanna. How's it going?"

"Good." She held up the champagne bottle. "Need a refill?"

"You know it." She pushed her glass and Amelia's over to Hanna. "Top them both off, please."

"Oh, no. None for me." Amelia gave Holly a WTF look. She knew Amelia couldn't drink.

"Relax, they're both for me," Holly said and winked at Amelia. "I need to rehydrate after all that dancing."

"Right. Because that's how it works," Amelia teased.

But the truth was that Amelia was jealous she couldn't join in. She loved champagne, but sacrifices had to be made when one was pregnant.

Before she knew it, Amelia was surrounded by happy couples. While the newlyweds, Brian and Shannon, were likely off consummating their marriage in a closet somewhere, Rex had followed Holly over and taken a seat. And they had attracted Yvette and Jacob, followed by Abby and Clay, and Wanda and Cameron. Couples were everywhere. Wasn't anyone in Keating Hollow single? She was beginning to seriously doubt it.

They all started gossiping at once. Yvette and Jacob had just submitted their final paperwork to adopt, Abby chattered about how much she loved being pregnant, and Wanda told them all about the house she and Cameron were planning to build.

At any other time in her life, she would have been thrilled to not only listen, but to actively engage in all of their good news. Amelia normally loved weddings and babies, and she'd played matchmaker to more than a couple of friends. There was no denying she was a romantic at heart. In fact, she was the person who watched holiday romances on television starting in October and only stopped in January when the programing turned to mysteries.

Unfortunately, she'd had her heart broken a few months prior, and she still hadn't recovered. Part of the issue was that she'd be carrying the evidence of that relationship for another five months, so it was hard to forget about him.

"Amelia, have you started working on your nursery yet?" Abby asked her, scooting over closer so they didn't have to yell over the din of the party.

"I have." Amelia felt a smile tug at her lips and all of the tension drain from her shoulders. For all of the angst she had about Grayson, she was always happy to talk about her pregnancy journey. "I just can't stop stenciling the walls."

"She's not kidding," Rex called from across the table. "My sister has created an entire zoo for that kid."

Amelia chuckled and rested her hands on her small baby bump. "I can't help it. I get started painting and time just flies."

"Ha. That's how I get when I'm in my studio working on new formulas or lotions," Abby said. "Listen, if you want to get together sometime soon and talk baby gear, I'd love a pre-delivery play date for just us moms. What do you think?"

"I'd love to." Amelia meant every word, too. She liked Abby Townsend. And if Amelia played her cards right, she might even get a golf cart race out of the deal.

Eventually, Amelia extracted herself from the Happyville table and returned to the chocolate bar. As she ate more than her fair share of chocolate covered caramels, she spotted Shannon's brother, Silas Ansell, and his boyfriend, Levi, on the dance floor. They were slow dancing and looked just as in love as the couples she'd left back at her table. Beside them, Cam Berry and his girlfriend, Blake, were trying, but they kept stepping on each other's feet. Each time it happened they'd crack up with laughter.

Her heart soared as she watched everyone. That was what love was supposed to look like. Not booty calls and promises to not get attached. She gritted her teeth just thinking about that stupid pact she'd made with Grayson. Well, the joke was on her, because she'd definitely gotten attached.

"Amelia?"

She could have sworn just thinking about him made her hear his voice. She shook her head, trying to dislodge the memories that resided in there.

"Amelia," she heard again, and this time, she turned and spotted him coming right for her. She quickly glanced around for cover, just like she had in the gallery a couple of weeks earlier, only now it was worse than foolish. He'd already spotted her. It wasn't as if she could just dive under a table.

"Grayson," she gasped out. "What are you doing here?"

"I work here," he said, looking sexier than ever in his basic black wool pants and fitted, white button-down shirt. He oozed sex appeal with his wide shoulders, narrow hips, delicious eight pack, and that damn dimple that always did things to her that she couldn't talk about.

"I mean what are you doing here at the wedding, not—" She clamped her mouth shut, realizing that he'd said he worked there. There where? The vineyard or Keating Hollow?

"Oh, Brian invited me," he said. "We met at the brewpub and hit it off. He said this would be the party of the year, and it looks like he's not wrong."

"Working where?" she asked. "Here at the winery or here in Keating Hollow?"

"Here on the West Coast. I'm an account rep for a distributor that works with restaurants that carry locally crafted beer, wine, and ciders. The Townsends are one of my clients."

When Amelia was too shocked to say anything, he continued. "I heard you were working in Keating Hollow, so I came to town a few weeks ago to see you, but it turns out you're a hard girl to pin down. I was sorry I missed you. You look incredible. All soft and lush and… damn, now I want you. Like always." He gave her that sexy half grin that never failed to tempt her into his bed.

But not this time. This time she'd be strong.

He moved until he was right behind her and placed a hand on her thigh. Her body started to tingle to life with pure anticipation.

"I had a vision that you'd be in my bed tonight," he whispered in her ear.

Desire rippled up her spine, and she almost caved right then and there, but there was no way she could go back to his room right then. Not before they talked. "That's funny. My vision was of me alone in my oversized bathtub with lots of bubbles."

He eyed her suspiciously. "You don't have visions."

"I do now." She smiled sweetly at him because it was true. And also distressing. She had no idea how people with visions functioned.

"But how?" He frowned. "You're a fire witch, not a spirit witch. I've never heard of that before."

"It happens sometimes to pregnant women," she said, her voice shaking as she got the words out. There. She'd said it.

Grayson froze and then slowly lowered his gaze down her body. "Are you saying what I think you're saying?"

Amelia placed her hands on her belly, forcing her silky dress to show her baby bump. "Congratulations, Grayson. You're going to be a daddy in about five months."

DEANNA'S BOOK LIST

Witches of Keating Hollow:

Soul of the Witch
Heart of the Witch
Spirit of the Witch
Dreams of the Witch
Courage of the Witch
Love of the Witch
Power of the Witch
Essence of the Witch
Muse of the Witch
Vision of the Witch

Witches of Christmas Grove:

A Witch For Mr. Holiday
A Witch For Mr. Christmas

Premonition Pointe Novels:

Witching For Grace
Witching For Hope

Witching For Joy

Jade Calhoun Novels:

Haunted on Bourbon Street
Witches of Bourbon Street
Demons of Bourbon Street
Angels of Bourbon Street
Shadows of Bourbon Street
Incubus of Bourbon Street
Bewitched on Bourbon Street
Hexed on Bourbon Street
Dragons of Bourbon Street

Pyper Rayne Novels:

Spirits, Stilettos, and a Silver Bustier
Spirits, Rock Stars, and a Midnight Chocolate Bar
Spirits, Beignets, and a Bayou Biker Gang
Spirits, Diamonds, and a Drive-thru Daiquiri Stand
Spirits, Spells, and Wedding Bells

Ida May Chronicles:

Witched To Death
Witch, Please
Stop Your Witchin'

Crescent City Fae Novels:

Influential Magic
Irresistible Magic
Intoxicating Magic

Last Witch Standing:

Bewitched by Moonlight

Soulless at Sunset
Bloodlust By Midnight
Bitten At Daybreak

Witch Island Brides:
The Wolf's New Year Bride
The Vampire's Last Dance
The Warlock's Enchanted Kiss
The Shifter's First Bite

Destiny Novels:
Defining Destiny
Accepting Fate

Wolves of the Rising Sun:
Jace
Aiden
Luc
Craved
Silas
Darien
Wren

Black Bear Outlaws:
Cyrus
Chase
Cole

Bayou Springs Alien Mail Order Brides:
Zeke
Gunn
Echo

ABOUT THE AUTHOR

New York Times and USA Today bestselling author, Deanna Chase, is a native Californian, transplanted to the slower paced lifestyle of southeastern Louisiana. When she isn't writing, she is often goofing off with her husband in New Orleans or playing with her two shih tzu dogs. For more information and updates on newest releases visit her website at deannachase.com.

ww.ingramcontent.com/pod-product-compliance
ning Source LLC
rsburg PA
0402210626
00006BB/2093
7 8 1 9 4 0 2 9 9 9 9 0 *